# Fantasy paled

Caroline had never gone so far as to imagine the way her inner wrists would feel on his shoulders, or the way his chest would press closer with each breath, or the way his thighs would brace hers.

Soft. Moist. Sweet. Brendan couldn't believe how perfect she was. Caroline… He didn't stop to ask himself if he was rushing things when he sought her mouth. Her lips were waiting and parted.

Details blurred then into an aura of overall bliss. Mouths, tongues, hands, bodies— slow, languorous movements gradually speeding up with their sensual demands. There was heat within heat. And the fine line between fantasy and reality ceased to exist....

**Barbara Delinsky** never seems to run out of unusual and evocative story ideas. She has the unique ability to use her own life experience and her background in sociology and psychology to create wonderful fantasies. *Heat Wave* is a prime example. In fact, the heroine is a psychologist and the hero is a lawyer—much like Barbara and her attorney husband.

## Books by Barbara Delinsky

FINGER PRINTS
WITHIN REACH

### HARLEQUIN TEMPTATION

### HARLEQUIN INTRIGUE

# *Heat Wave*

## BARBARA DELINSKY

# *Harlequin Books*

TORONTO • NEW YORK • LONDON
AMSTERDAM • PARIS • SYDNEY • HAMBURG
STOCKHOLM • ATHENS • TOKYO • MILAN

Published October 1987

ISBN 0-373-25273-0

Printed in Canada

# 1

CAROLINE COOPER untied the wilting bow at the neck of her blouse, released its top button and peeled the damp fabric from her sweaty neck.

*Beep.* "You're working too late, Caroline. It's eight o'clock your time now, and Lord knows when you'll be hearing this message. . . . I'm worried about your father. The X rays of the leg look good, but he's in terrible pain. I'm beginning to wonder if he'll ever walk right, let alone play golf, and so help me, if he doesn't we'll sue. Maybe we'll sue anyway. The doctor who set his leg wrong last fall shouldn't be practicing medicine." Sigh. "Call me when you get a chance, sweetheart. We need to talk." *Click.*

Freeing the last of the buttons, Caroline carefully separated the blouse from her shoulders and arms.

*Beep.* "Ahh, Caroline, still out on the town. How I envy you your energy. Can you loan me a little?" Groan. "The baby's getting bigger. I'm getting bigger. Where I get the strength to keep going I'll never know. I think it's defiance. The men in the firm are worried that I'll give birth in the office. What sissies they are. Of course, they've never been pregnant. For that matter, neither have you, but I need a pep talk. Call whenever." *Click.*

Caroline breathed a sigh of relief when she stepped out of her skirt and an even greater one when she rolled the nylons from her legs.

*Beep.* "Would you like to know what your good friend did today? She demanded—not asked but demanded— to keep the lake house. It's not enough that she has the Colonial, the Camaro and Amy. She's a greedy bitch. I don't know what you ever saw in her as a friend." Grunt. "I don't know what I ever saw in her as a wife." Pause. "Catch you another time, Sis." *Click.*

Clad in panties and bra, Caroline padded wearily to the bathroom. The light there was oppressive after the dimness of the larger room and, if anything, exaggerated the heat. Wetting a cool cloth, she pressed it to her face.

Flowers. That was what she wanted to come home to after a long day's work. A bouquet of fresh, sweet-smelling flowers. Not an answering machine spouting complaints.

With a sigh, she dragged the cloth down over her neck and held it to her pulse. A bouquet of flowers...or a bunch of brightly colored balloons...or a gorgeous guy with a sympathetic smile and a frozen daiquiri in his outstretched hand. She moved the cloth around to her nape and realized that just then she'd take the daiquiri over the guy.

With a wistful sigh this time, she unsnapped her bra and let it fall to the commode before rewetting the cloth and dragging it slowly over those parts of her that hadn't breathed all day—the insides of her elbows, the curve of her waistline, beneath and between her breasts. The relief was wonderful, if short-lived. She debated taking a cool shower, decided it was too great an effort. She felt drained. What she wanted—given no bouquet of flowers, no bunch of balloons, no gorgeous guy, no frozen daiquiri—was to wipe her mind clear of all thought and relax.

Dropping the cloth in the sink, she flipped off the light and returned to the large single room she called home. It was a loft apartment, the third and top floor of a Georgetown town house. She'd been working in Washington for three years before she'd found it. Miracle of miracles, she'd been able to afford the rent, so the last thing she'd begrudged was the lack of air conditioning.

Until tonight. The dog days of summer had arrived suddenly and with a vengeance, but it wasn't even summer. It was the sixth of June. She shuddered to think what July and August would be like.

Her movements were sluggish, legs seeming to lack the strength to cut through the opaque heat. The Casablanca fan on the ceiling stirred the air some, but because the only air in the room was sweltering, the improvement was negligible. Her feet made a sticky sound on the large adobe tiles as she crossed to the closet. Even the thin batiste shift she slipped on felt heavy.

Opening the broad French windows as far as they'd go, she put one knee on the window seat, gathered the mass of her thick hair in her hands and held it off her neck. The courtyard seemed devoid of air this night. Still, it was peaceful—another plus for the loft. Cars were parked around the cobblestone drive; at its center was a small cluster of trees and shrubs, a patch of grass and a modest wrought-iron bench. Sharing the courtyard on its far side were town houses just like hers. All in all, the effect was charming.

Or claustrophobic. She'd begun thinking of open spaces, of fields filled with wheat that swayed in the wind or meadows dotted with willows and irrigated with bubbling brooks, when the sound of the telephone rent the still night air. She closed her eyes for a minute, took a long, deep breath and pushed away from the seat. Her hand hovered over the phone in a moment's indecision before it finally lowered.

"Hello?"

"Hello, yourself," came a pleasant male voice. "Just get in?"

She didn't know whether to be relieved or annoyed. Though she'd been dating Elliot for several months, she wasn't in the mood for him just then. She was hot and tired. After a long day of talk, she craved silence. Still, she supposed Elliot was better than her family.

"A few minutes ago. What's up?"

"It's been a hell of a day, but I'm in heaven now. No more than two hours ago, we signed the contract on the shopping mall, but you wouldn't have believed the last-minute glitches. It was touch and go for so long I thought the whole thing was going down the tubes. But we did it, we actually did it. Do you realize what a coup this is?"

Caroline gave a weak smile as she daubed her beading forehead with the back of her hand. Predictably, Elliot babbled on.

"My firm is about to build the classiest mall Arlington's ever seen. For a young firm, that's not bad. The developer may be a tough nut to crack, but the architectural plans are great, and our reputation's bound to soar. So—" he paused and spoke with an audible smile "—how about you and I go out for some champagne and caviar?"

The frozen daiquiri still sounded better. She closed her eyes and let her head fall back, bracing the lax muscles of her neck with her hand. "I'm really exhausted, Elliot."

"But there's cause for celebration. It's not every day I land a deal like this."

"Shouldn't you be celebrating with your partners?"

"Spent the last hour doing that. The next couple of hours are for us."

She stifled a moan and worked at summoning compassion. "I'd really love to, but it's been a hell of a day for me, too, and I don't have a contract to show for it."

"Come out with me and I'll share the excitement."

"Nah. I'd only drag you down."

"Sweetheart," he drawled, "that would be impossible. Nothing's about to drag me down tonight. I'm on a first-class high. Join me and you'll see."

She rubbed an incipient tension from the bridge of her nose. "Thanks, but I'd better take a rain check."

"Rain checks aren't offered on bright nights like this. Who knows how long the high will last? Once the reality of the job sets in, I'll be a nervous wreck. Now's the time to celebrate."

She sighed. "Elliot, I don't think I could hold my head up for long in a restaurant."

"Then take a cab over here and we'll do it big with take-out or something."

"I'm not dressed."

"So much the better," he said in a tone that immediately told her she'd said the wrong thing. He'd been making suggestive noises for the past few weeks, and she'd held him off with one gentle quip after another. It wasn't that she didn't like him; she did. He was a good conversationalist and he was polite. He enjoyed concerts, lectures, fine restaurants. She could forgive him his self-centeredness, because she understood that it came from insecurity. But she felt little for him beyond friendship. He didn't turn her on.

"We'll have dinner another night," she said.

"I'd offer to bring food over there, but your place is probably hot as hell. What if I come rescue you, myself? You must be dying."

"I'm fine, just very tired."

He was quiet for a moment. By the time he spoke again, he'd apparently acclimated himself to Caroline's refusal, because there was a jauntiness in his voice. "You're missing out on a good thing."

"I know. Forgive me?"

"Don't I always?" he countered with such flippancy that she wanted to scream. But she didn't have the strength. Or the heart.

"Yes, Elliot."

"We're on for Saturday, aren't we?"

"Uh-huh."

"Okay, sweetheart. I'll talk with you later, then."

"Right."

"Think of me tonight?"

She left that one alone. "I'm really glad you got the project, Elliot."

"So am I. Bye-bye."

Replacing the receiver in its cradle, she stood for a minute with her head bowed, rubbing the throbbing spot between her eyes. It occurred to her that with increasing frequency Elliot make her throb that way. Too bad the spot was wrong.

Rolling her eyes at the twist of her thoughts, she made for the refrigerator and a pitcher of iced tea. She'd no sooner grasped the handle, though, when there was a knock at her door. Reluctantly closing the refrigerator, she shuffled across the room and put her eye to the peephole. The cone-shaped face with an absurdly large nose in the lead was that of her downstairs neighbor.

She opened the door with a smile. "Hi, Connie." Her eyes widened. "You look super." Freed from the distortion of the peephole lens, Connie Halpern's face was exceptionally pretty, but Caroline had already known that. What impressed her now was the chic and daringly cut lounging outfit Connie wore. But then, Caroline shouldn't have been surprised. Connie was forty-two and divorced. A small designer boutique in Georgetown Park kept her busy by day. A congressman from Idaho kept her busy by night. "Big date?"

"Mmm. And I promised him *café kirsch*," Connie answered with a grimace, "but I'm out of eggs. You don't...by chance..." Her eyes finished the sentence by wandering toward the wall that was Caroline's kitchen.

"Sure do," Caroline said. "How many?" she called over her shoulder as she returned to the refrigerator.

Connie was right behind her. "Two, if you have them. Whew, is it hot up here! What's wrong with the air conditioning?"

"There isn't any."

"Why not?" Connie asked with endearing indignance.

"Ask Nestor Realty."

"The creeps. My place is delightfully cool." She took the eggs from Caroline. "I'd invite you down, but . . ."

"You have a special guest and I look like something the cat dragged home."

"Actually," Connie said, tipping her head and giving Caroline a good once-over, "you look kind of sexy. Where's Elliot?"

"Home."

"Oh."

Caroline smiled again and gave her friend a nudge. "Go on. He's waiting."

But Connie just stood. "I feel guilty as hell leaving you up here alone and sweltering."

"Alone I don't mind, and as for sweltering, it's really not that bad. I was just about to help myself to a tall glass of iced tea when you knocked."

That was enough to let Connie off the hook. "Go to it, then, girl," she said, heading for the door. "And thanks for the eggs. You're a lifesaver." With a wave, she was gone.

Closing the door behind her, Caroline promptly poured the drink she'd promised herself. No sooner had she replaced the pitcher in the refrigerator, though, when the phone rang. She stared at it, wishing she had the nerve to either ignore it or unplug it. But the caller could be her mother again, this time in a real panic. Or her sister, Karen, saying that she'd gone into premature labor. Or there might be an emergency involving one of her clients.

"Hello?"

"Caroline?"

Her pulse faltered at the familiarity of the voice. It had been six months since she'd last heard it, but when one had been intimately involved with a man for over a year, there were certain things one didn't forget. Like his voice. And the promises he'd made . . . and those he'd broken.

"Ben."

"How are you?"

"Just fine," she said. Actually, she was trying to figure that one out. The initial sound of his voice had touched off a reaction, but it seemed to have been more one of surprise than anything else.

"I'm back in town."

"Oh?"

"Uh-huh. I finished up in Madrid."

Benjamin Howe was a floating member of the diplomatic corps. Only after the fact had Caroline realized that he manipulated his assignments to coincide with his love life. Or vice versa.

"How was it?" she asked, plucking uncomfortably at those parts of her shift that were clinging to her skin.

"Interesting. But it's good to be home. Tell me about you. What have you been up to?"

She shrugged. "Same old thing, Ben."

"Still counseling?"

"It's my field."

He paused as though trying to think of something else to say. Or waiting for her to pick up the ball. Eventually he asked, "Have you had any interesting cases lately?"

"They're all interesting."

"I mean, anything out of the ordinary?"

"Unfortunately, broken homes aren't out of the ordinary nowadays. Neither are disturbed children, unfortunately."

"Fortunately for you, or you'd be out of business."

She tried to take his words for the humor she knew he'd intended, but still they sounded crass. She was beginning to feel uncomfortable in ways that had nothing to do with her stifling apartment. Ben, who'd once fascinated her with his good looks and exciting position, no longer did. She wasn't sure why he'd called.

"I'd be very happy to be out of business," she said, "if it meant there was less unhappiness in the world, just as I'm sure an oncologist would be thrilled by a cure for cancer."

"Ah, so lofty."

"No. But I do mean what I say."

There was a long pause, then a quiet "Touché."

Caroline's lips formed the reluctant beginnings of a smile. Ben had always been astute to the nuances of words. It was necessary in his work. Apparently he hadn't lost his touch while he'd been in Spain.

"You're still angry at me," he decided. If his perceptiveness was off just a hair, it was because he couldn't see her indulgent expression.

"No." She'd grown a lot since she and Ben had broken up. "I'm not angry."

"But you haven't forgotten."

"No woman forgets promises of undying love. That doesn't mean she has to wither and die when the promises are broken."

"So you've moved on? That has to say something about the love you felt for me."

"I never said that I loved you. Not once."

In the lengthy silence that followed, Caroline tugged open a kitchen drawer, took out an elastic band and, balancing the phone between jaw and shoulder, scooped her hair into a high, makeshift ponytail. The ends were wet. Her neck was even wetter. She wanted that iced tea. She wanted the window seat. She wanted peace and quiet.

"No, you never did say that, did you?" Ben asked, then went on before she could agree. "But, look, I didn't call to rehash the past. I just thought it'd be fun to get together. How about a drink? For old times' sake, if nothing else."

"Tonight?"

"Sure."

"Uh, thanks, Ben, but I'm beat. Maybe another time."

"How about tomorrow?"

She shook her head. "Late meetings."

"Then Friday. I could meet you after work."

"I'm sorry, but I have other plans." Opening the freezer, she dropped several ice cubes in her drink, holding one out to rub on her neck.

"You really are seeing someone else?"

"You could say that," she said with a touch of humor. The ice felt good, though it was melting on contact.

"Anyone I know?"

"I hope not. That'd be pretty uncomfortable, comparing notes and all."

"Is he good?"

"At what?"

"You know."

She hesitated for only the short amount of time it took to straighten her spine. "And you don't. Why don't we leave it at that?"

"You're trying to make me jealous. It won't work, Caroline. I know what we had, and it'd be pretty hard to beat."

Caroline heard his defensiveness and surprised herself by feeling remorse. Then again, she should have expected it. She was a softy at heart. Ben had always prided himself on his sexual prowess. Teasing him about finding a replacement was hitting below the belt in more ways than one.

"I'm not denying what we had," she conceded. "It was good while it lasted. But it's over."

"So what's the harm in going out for a drink?"

"Maybe another time. Listen, I'm really glad you're back. I hope things go well."

"What's his name?"

"Who?"

"Whoever you're seeing."

She debated telling him to mind his own business, but she knew Ben too well for that. He was persistent. When he set his mind to something, he usually got it. He'd wanted her and he'd gotten her. He'd wanted out and he'd gotten out. If he wanted back in now, for whatever his reasons, she was going to have to close the door in his face.

The problem was that she wasn't naturally cruel or vengeful. She didn't want to hurt him; she simply wanted to be free of him. And the best way to do that, she realized, was to paint herself as being unavailable.

She could lie and say that she was wildly in love with another man, even engaged to be married, but she'd never been good at lying. On the other hand, she wasn't opposed to presenting the facts and letting him jump to conclusions.

"His name is Elliot Markham. He's a builder. We've been seeing each other for nearly four months."

"Is it serious?"

Certainly not, she reflected. But if Elliot was to serve as a buffer, she couldn't be that blunt. So she said, "Give me a few more months, then ask me again. I'm being cautious this time around."

"I see. Well—" he sighed "—maybe I'll call you another time and we'll have that drink."

Persistence. There it was again. Or maybe it was pride. Ben didn't like being refused. Of course, chances were that before "another time" rolled around, he'd find another woman. Knowing Ben, she mused wryly, he'd invite her for the drink anyway and then have his new lady friend pick him up afterward.

"We'll see. Take care, Ben."

"You, too, Caroline."

This time when she hung up the phone, she did switch on the answering machine. There was something deceitful about doing that, but she was just hot and tired enough to stoop to deceit. She'd about had it with phone calls.

Ben. Of all people, she'd never expected to hear from him. Six months before, he'd made his plans without telling her, then hadn't looked back when he'd left. She'd been stunned and deeply hurt. Anger had eventually set in, but relief had followed. Ben wasn't right for her. She'd been too involved in the relationship to see it at the time, but it never would have worked. His phone call proved how thoroughly she was over him. And Elliot . . . well, she was grateful to have had him in the wings.

The ice cube she'd held was nothing more than lingering streaks of wetness on her neck, forehead and cheeks. Taking the glass of tea from the counter, she settled on the window seat with her shoulder and head braced against the wooden jamb. She tried to concentrate on the small stirrings of air, but there were few. The night was a thick blanket of heat. Little moved or breathed.

Unable to draw her mind into a total blank, she found herself thinking of life's little complications. There was her work, for one thing. On the plus side was her love of it. She was in partnership with three other therapists; their offices were in newly renovated and comfortable quarters within walking distance of her apartment. When she'd first joined the practice, she'd assumed that her work would consist of references from her partners, who'd already established themselves in the area. And indeed, that was how she'd started. But one client had led to another, and to a consulting position at a local prep school, and to leadership of a group session, and to more clients. Her practice was full, evenly split between children and adults. She found it incredibly rewarding.

There were days like today, though, when things just hadn't worked. Her eight-o'clock appointment, a trou-

bled high-school junior, had stood her up. Her eleven-
o'clock appointment, a woman struggling to make her
marriage work, had spent the hour evading issues of de-
pendency by asking how Caroline could possibly understand what she was going through if she'd never been
married herself. Her three-o'clock appointment, a ten-
year-old girl, refused to talk. And her four-o'clock appointment, a divorced pair whose two children she was
also counseling, skirted every pertinent issue by accusing her of a conflict of interest in working with the whole
family. It didn't matter that they'd been the ones to ini-
tially request it; when the therapist herself became a
negative factor in the proceedings, the prognosis was
poor. Though Caroline had promptly referred the parents to one of her partners, she'd been saddened by the
loss of therapy time and effort.

After swirling the ice cubes around in her glass, she
took several sips of tea. The drink soothed her throat but
did little to cool her thoughts. Frustration at work was
part of the job. Even on the best of days, the intense concentration she gave her patients was draining. Still, when
four setbacks occurred in an eight-hour span, she was
discouraged.

A trickle of sweat crept into the hollow between her
breasts. She dabbed at it lightly with her shift, then,
prying the undersides of her thighs from the seat, drew
up her knees into a more comfortable pose.

It was the responsibility that was so awesome, she decided. Clients came to her with issues of mental health.
When she let them down, she felt let down herself. Which
was pretty much why, she mused as she cast a glance at
the telephone, she felt guilty about the answering machine. She had a responsibility toward her family, too.

Wishing she could be a little more selfish, she set down her tea, went to turn off the machine, then returned to her perch. How could she say no when they wanted to talk? She might not be the alarmist her mother was, but if her mother felt in a panic, then the panic was real. Likewise, she could remind her sister that no one had forced her to juggle a marriage, a law career and a pregnancy, but still she was proud of Karen and had encouraged her from the start. And as for her brother, Carl, her sadness over his pending divorce was made all the worse by her fondness for his wife, Diane, and the knowledge that she'd been the one to originally bring the two together.

Little complications? She supposed. But they weighed her down. From the time she'd reached her teens, she'd been the Dear Abby of the family. Just as she couldn't heal her father's leg, erase her mother's worries, ease the burden of pregnancy for Karen or miraculously mend Carl's marital wounds, she couldn't turn a deaf ear to their pleas.

She gave a great sigh, then a tiny moan. Her shift was quickly growing damp from perspiration. Leaning forward, she peeled the light fabric from her back, gave a lethargic twist, then returned to her position against the window frame. She straightened each leg in turn to wipe moisture from the creases behind her knees. Then, planting her feet flat and apart, she gathered the short hem of her shift and tucked it with some decorum between her legs.

One part of her wished she'd taken Elliot up on his offer of air-conditioned solace, but the greater, saner part knew she'd made the right decision. She and Elliot were on their last leg as a couple. He wanted sex; she didn't. If that little complication hadn't cropped up, they might

have continued a while longer in a pleasant relationship. But it was only a matter of time before he pushed
the issue too far. She would be as tactful as possible, but
there was no way she'd go to bed with him out of pity.

Breaking off was going to be awkward. Elliot happened to be the brother of one of her partners. Another
little complication. And now Ben had popped back into
the Washington scene, apparently willing to pick up
where he'd left off. So she needed Elliot a while longer.
But she hated to use him that way. She hated it.

With another soft moan, she shifted languidly on the
window seat. Sweat trickled down her neck. She pushed
it back up with a finger that tangled in loose tendrils of
hair fallen from her ponytail. When the wisps fell right
back down and clung damply to her nape, she left them
alone. Closing her eyes, she tipped her head toward the
night and raised the glass of tea to her neck in the hope
that the condensation would cool her heated skin.

Then she opened her eyes and saw him—a stranger,
far across the courtyard. He was sprawled on the tiny fire
escape just beyond his own third-floor window. The
night was dark, but the pale golden glow from his apartment outlined his shape, and she couldn't look away.

His hair was thick, spiked damply on his brow. His
legs were long, lean and firm, bent at the knees and
spread much like hers. He had large shoulders, one
slightly lower than the other as he propped his weight on
a hand. The other hand dangled over his knee, fingers
circling what she assumed to be a beer can. Other than
a pair of brief shorts, his body was bare.

Caroline had no idea who he was or where he'd come
from. Though she knew her immediate neighbors, his
row of town houses faced a different street. She wouldn't
have passed him coming or going, and since she didn't

own a car, she wouldn't have bumped into him in the courtyard.

She'd never seen anyone on the fire escape before, not that she'd done a lot of looking. Only the heat had brought her to her window tonight; she wondered if it had been the same for him.

With fifty feet of night separating them, she couldn't see his face. But she wanted to. She wanted to see his eyes, or at least his expression, which would be telling. She imagined that he was every bit as hot as she was, and every bit as tired. Was he as frustrated with the little complications in life? Was he feeling the brunt of a million demands? Was he, too, wishing he could escape from it all for a time?

There were no answers to her questions, of course. He was an unknown, a man she had little likelihood of actually meeting. The pace of life in the capital kept people on the move and wasn't at all conducive to leisurely run-ins.

But he was at the right place at the right time. She needed an escape, an outlet for secret thoughts. Features softening in a shy and feminine way, she tipped her head a bit more and gave vent to her fantasies.

He'd be tall. At five-seven, she needed a man who topped six feet. She liked feeling petite and protected, though she hadn't had much experience in being either. She'd always been the protector, it seemed. Granted, it was a psychological distinction, but it wouldn't hurt to set the stage right.

He'd be dark. She fancied that their coloring would be similar. She rather liked the idea that people might take them for brother and sister, while they shared secret smiles at the truth. Her own hair was dark brown, often mistaken for black. His would be the same. And it would be on the long side. There was something rakish about a man with long hair. She could see that it was thick, because it capped his head well, but the shadows on his neck hid its length. Which was okay, because she was only dreaming.

He'd be handsome. His features would be well-defined and boldly cut, giving him a distinctly aristocratic look. Mmm. An aristocratic look. She liked that. She'd never mingled with the aristocracy. Her parents were solidly upper middle-class, but aristocratic? Not quite. Not that she had aspirations of running with the hounds or boogying with the jet set. She'd be bored to death—not to mention the fact that she thought the hunt was cruel and discos gave her a headache. Still, it'd be nice to know that he could have had that and had opted out.

But she was getting away from looks, and she hadn't finished with handsome. His nose would be straight, his cheeks lean, his jaw firm and his lips expressive. She could read a lot in people's lips—relaxed or tight set, chewed or sucked or pursed, curved up or down or drawn into straight lines. Not that she'd have to rely on his mouth to convey his feelings, because he'd have the deepest, most inviting and eloquent brown eyes.

The last thought surprised her. She had brown eyes. She'd never thought them particularly gorgeous. But his would be, she knew, because of all that went along with them.

Oh, and he'd have a heavy five-o'clock shadow. That was because he'd just come in from work or from running. She pictured him a runner. Of course, if he were coming to pick her up, he'd shower and shave first. He'd want to look his best for her. She'd have to tell him that he looked fantastic all grubby and sweaty.

She brought the glass of tea to her cheek and rubbed wet against wet. Tall, dark and handsome. That was what he'd be. People would look at them when they passed, thinking what a stunning couple they made.

She smiled in self-mockery. She wasn't stunning. Attractive, yes. But with him, she'd be stunning. Or she'd feel it, and that would be all that mattered.

Having dispensed with physical attributes, she moved on to other vital statistics. He'd be in his late thirties, just about right for her thirty-one years. She wanted someone older than she was, someone more experienced. If he was in his late thirties, even early forties, he'd be well established in his chosen field. He'd be successful, of course, but more important than that, he'd be confident. She needed a confident man, because she was, overall, a confident woman. She was also introspective and insightful, qualities that intimidated a man who was less sure of himself.

She intimidated Elliot, who compensated by artificially inflating his strengths and successes. To some extent she'd intimidated Ben. At least, she'd assumed that was what she'd done, because she couldn't find any other reason why he'd always felt the need to come on so forcefully. She was by nature a watcher and a listener; when she spoke, she had something pertinent to say. Some men found that to be a threat.

He wouldn't. He'd be a strong man but one who welcomed her opinions. He'd appreciate the fact that she thought about things, that she was fascinated by her own motives and those of others. He'd be able to listen without getting defensive. At the same time, he'd be able to offer his own opinions without insisting that they were law.

Open-minded. She figured that summed it up. He'd be open-minded, thoughtful and intelligent. His career? She straightened one leg on the seat and flexed her toes while she thought about that for a minute. He'd have to be in a caring profession. A doctor? Perhaps. Maybe a psychiatrist. That way they'd be able to bounce cases off each other. Then again, many of the psychiatrists she knew were weird. Chalk psychiatrist and put in teacher. Mmm, that idea appealed to her. He'd be involved with kids. Maybe college kids. She had her share of clients from local colleges and found her work with them to be particularly rewarding. They wanted help. They could respond.

She brushed her arm over her forehead, pushing back damp strands of hair. The stranger didn't move, other than to occasionally take a drink from the can he held. It was a light beer, she decided. He wasn't really a drinker, but he needed something to quench his thirst and beer was the best. Light beer, because he didn't want to develop a beer belly, though he was more health conscious than vain.

Health conscious was a good thing to be at his age. It was a good thing to be at any age, but if he was approaching his forties, it was all the more important.

She paused for an instant as a new thought struck. If he was nearly forty, tall, dark, handsome, self-confident, successful and caring, there had to be good reason why he wasn't married. Because he wasn't. She didn't fool with married men. Besides, if his apartment mirrored hers, it wasn't suitable for two.

Perhaps he was divorced. He may have married young and none too wisely—she'd forgive him that early innocence—then redeemed himself by ending the union before two lives, or more, were ruined.

Maybe he'd never married at all. He'd been too involved in his career. Or—she rather liked this idea—he'd been waiting for the right woman to come along.

*Well, Tall-Dark-and-Handsome, here I am.* But she didn't have to tell him that. He'd know. One glance and he'd know. She wasn't looking her best just then, but that wouldn't matter to him. He'd want her for better or for worse. And worse wasn't all that bad. Hadn't Connie said she looked sexy?

Well, Caroline decided with a fanciful sigh, so did he. There he was on his fire escape, tired and sweaty and, really, when she came right down to it, not much more than a full-bodied shadow. Still, she imagined that he was sexy as hell. True, her opinion was tinged by everything else she'd conjured up, but since she was into the fantasy, she'd do it right.

He'd be the epitome of raw masculinity. One look at him close up and she'd feel those awakening tingles deep inside. She tried to remember when she'd felt them last. It might have been with Ben, at the beginning, when she'd been snowed by his style. Or it might have been with Jonathan Carey, her first and only other lover, but she suspected that what she'd felt then had had more to do with the excitement of being a freshman in college and finally "doing it." Then again, the last time she'd felt those tingles, really felt them, might have been when she was seventeen and necking in Greg O'Malley's Mustang. When Greg had grazed her breasts, her insides had come to life. It had all been so new then—new and mysterious and forbidden.

It would be new with Tall-Dark-and-Handsome, too. New as in mind-boggling, heart stopping and soul reaching. He would be a stupendous lover. Caroline could see it in the way he held himself. His body was well tuned and coordinated. Ropy shoulders, tight hips, long, lean legs . . . sexy . . . oh, Lord . . .

She clamped her thighs together and took a shaky breath, a little shocked by her physical reaction to thoughts alone. And just then, in that moment of reality's intrusion, she noticed something. The profile of the dark stranger across the courtyard had changed. He'd turned his head. He was looking at her.

Her heartbeat tripped. A flush spread over her cheeks, deepening that already created by the heat. For a split second she feared that he knew all she'd been thinking. She wondered how long he'd been looking at her and wondered why she hadn't noticed sooner. Perhaps because it was normal for a man to look at a woman when they were making love?

But the fantasy was over and still he looked. She averted her gaze for a minute, then looked right back. Her embarrassment eased. Her chin came up a notch. She knew that he couldn't possibly know her thoughts. And if he did, what of it? She was an adult. She was free to dream as she saw fit.

That brought her to the fantasy's bottom line. She would be swept off her feet by Tall-Dark-and-Handsome, swept up, up and away from the hassles of her life, but there would be no strings attached. She could come and go as she pleased. She would feel neither responsibility nor guilt. No restrictions. No little complications.

It sounded divine.

But there was another sound just then. She swung her head around. Her telephone. She glanced back at the stranger. He didn't move. The phone rang again. She wasn't sure whether he could hear the ring, but on the chance that he could, she had to answer it. Pushing herself up, she crossed the floor in resignation.

"Hello?"

"Gladys?" asked an elderly male voice.

"Excuse me?"

"Is this Gladys?"

She couldn't believe it. "You must have the wrong number."

"Oh," said the man, "I'm sorry."

*No problem,* she thought with a sigh as she hung up the phone. Her hand remained on the receiver for a minute, thumb rubbing across its smooth grip. Then, straightening her shoulders, she crossed to the side of the room where she would be out of sight. She ran her tongue over her bottom lip. She curved one hand around her neck. Then, trying to be—feel—nonchalant, she worked her way back to the window. When she reached it, she stopped. She took one baby step, then another. With her hand still on her neck in a thoughtful pose, she turned her head and peeked out.

He was gone.

# 2

CAROLINE RETURNED TO WORK the next morning feeling refreshed. A thunderstorm at midnight had brought relief from the heat. Thanks to the ceiling fan, her apartment had cooled nicely and she'd been able to get a solid seven hours of sleep. She didn't mind that the temperature was again on the rise. Her office was cool. She'd face the loft later.

Every one of her morning appointments showed up, and on time. There were several tough sessions, but nothing as frustrating as what she'd faced the day before. Given that bit of encouragement, she decided against running out for lunch. Instead, she sat at her desk, opened a carton of yogurt and put through a call to her mother, who had been at the back of her mind since she'd woken up. Experience told her that the guilt she felt about not calling sooner was worse than the call itself would be.

Naturally, there were explanations to be made; Madeline Cooper was slightly miffed. "I was hoping you'd call back last night, Caroline. I didn't get a wink of sleep."

"I'm sorry, Mother."

"You must have been out very late."

"I didn't get in until ten—"

"But that was only nine here. You could have called."

"—and I was exhausted," Caroline went on. "I wouldn't have been much good to you."

"You could have called and told me that. I spent the night worrying about you, on top of everything else."

Caroline might have reminded her mother that she was thirty-one, that she'd been away from home since the age of eighteen, that if something were desperately wrong the police would call—but it wasn't worth the effort. She had made each of the arguments before. She knew that she could make them until she was blue in the face and still her mother wouldn't hear.

So she changed the subject. "How's Dad?"

"Oh, he says he's all right, but I see him wince every time he moves." Her voice dropped to a mumble. "I'm sure there's something the doctors aren't telling us."

"I'm sorry, Mom. I didn't catch that."

"Hold on a second, dear. I'm going to pick up the phone in the den so I can sit comfortably."

Caroline could picture the scene; it was a recurring one. Her father was no doubt nearby, and her mother wanted privacy, which did not bode well for Madeline Cooper's frame of mind. That was nothing new.

"How are you doing, Caro?" came a deep, affection-ate voice.

"I'm fine, Dad. How about *you*? Leg aching?"

"Nothing I can't handle, despite what your mother says—"

"You can hang up now, Allan," Madeline shouted the instant she picked up the extension.

"Bye-bye, Daddy. We'll talk more another time."

"Sure thing, sweetheart." The line clicked.

"That's better," Madeline said. "I don't want to worry your father, but I do think the doctors are hiding some-thing."

"Why would they want to do that?"

"I don't know, but I feel it."

"You're imagining it, Mom. Believe me."

"Bone cancer. That would account for the pain, wouldn't it?"

"Dad does not have bone cancer."

"How do you know?"

"Because he broke his leg when he tripped in the garage. It was set wrong the first time, and now they've rebroken and reset it. There's the clear-cut cause of his pain."

"But you don't know it isn't cancer."

"Dad has seen more doctors in the past few months than he has in his entire life. They've taken blood and done a dozen other tests. If he had cancer, they'd know it. Doctors today are very cautious. They have their eyes wide open. My guess is they've ruled out everything from asthma to corns."

Madeline seemed momentarily pacified. "Still . . ."

"There's no 'still' about it. You're working with the best orthopedic team in the state. They're as sure of their work as any doctors can be. You said that the X rays were okay. Didn't they tell Dad to expect some pain?"

"Some pain I don't mind. Plenty of it, well, that's another story."

"Dad sounded fine to me." In fact, he'd sounded fine each time she'd spoken to him since the surgery, which was one of the reasons she felt so complacent.

"He tries to hide it, but I can see it in his face. It's difficult for him even to shift position."

"It'd be difficult for anyone with a full-leg cast. That thing's heavy."

"I suppose."

"Look at it this way, Mom. You know exactly what the problem is. We're talking bones here, not heart or lung or some other vital organ."

"But if he never walks right—"

"You don't know that that'll be so. The doctors have said that he'll spend six weeks in a cast, then another month or so in therapy. Wouldn't it be better to wait and see how things go before assuming the worst?"

"He's an active man, Caroline. You know that. If the leg doesn't heal right, his whole life-style will change."

"That's not *so*," Caroline insisted. She was trying to be patient, but after years of hearing the direst of dire predictions from her mother, her own patience was in short supply. She was by nature an optimist, very likely in reaction to Madeline's pessimism.

Tempering her voice, she projected the confidence she felt and that she knew her mother relied on. "The fact that Dad has always been active is to his benefit. He'll make the leg work by hook or by crook."

"And speaking of crooks," Madeline rushed on as though grateful for the lead, "I meant what I said last night. I'm seriously thinking of suing that first doctor."

"Wait, Mom. Just wait. See how you feel in two or three months. You may have a case for a lawsuit, but Karen would be the first one to tell you that a suit will take time and effort and money."

"We have a lawyer in the family."

Caroline had to laugh at that. "Good Lord, that's just what Karen needs. She's a corporate lawyer, not a litigator. And she's in Pennsylvania, not Wisconsin. *And* she's going to be slightly busy for the next eighteen years or so, or have you forgotten that you're about to be a grandmother?"

"I'm already a grandmother, but with the mess your brother's made of his marriage, it'll be a miracle if I get to see Amy once a year."

Which was another absurd comment, Caroline mused, but she didn't want to go into the issue of Carl's divorce, so she said, "Trust me, Mom. Dad will recover beautifully, and the two of you will be able to fly in often to see Karen and the baby, and Amy, for that matter." She paused. "Have you given any thought to what I suggested last week?"

"That I get a job? How can I get a job when your father needs me?"

"Dad has his own work, which he'll be getting back to as soon as he can manage with crutches." Caroline would have added that he'd do that much sooner if Madeline didn't hover so much, but she had to be tactful. "You need a diversion. We're all grown and away. Dad will be as active as ever. You should have gone to work years ago."

"We don't need the money."

"I know, but you'd feel better if you had something to take your mind off your worries."

"I can't think about that now," Madeline said, her words clipped. "Maybe later."

"I'll hold you to that," Caroline warned, then went on in a softer tone. "Would you feel better if I give the doctors a call?"

They were the magic words, just as Caroline had known they'd be. She could practically see her mother's face break into a relieved smile and could easily hear that relief in her voice. "Would you, sweetheart? I know how busy you are, but that would put my mind at ease. They don't listen to me," she complained, and, facetiously, Caroline wondered why not. "But they'd tell you the truth. They'd know that you couldn't be fooled. I have the number right here. Have you got a pencil?"

Caroline quickly scribbled the phone number her mother rattled off. "I'll put in a call now, but it may be a while before I reach one of them. Don't panic if I don't call right back, okay? It'll simply be because I haven't talked with them, not because they've said something I don't want you to know."

"You won't try to spare me?"

"Of course not, Mom."

"You'll call me either way?"

"Yes. And, Mom?"

"Yes, dear?"

"Try to relax. Dad is going to be just fine." Caroline looked up to catch the eye of one of her colleagues. "I've got to run now. I'll talk with you later."

She hung up the phone and tossed a glance skyward. "Role reversal. I sometimes forget who's the mother."

Pushing off from the doorjamb, Peter Hollis crossed the carpet to stand before her desk with his hands in his pockets and his legs planted wide. "Problems?"

"Nothing out of the ordinary."

"Good, 'cause I need your help."

"Uh-oh. Your group again?"

"Yeah. I have this seminar to give tonight, and if I don't spend some time preparing, I'm going to make an ass of myself."

Caroline could believe that. Peter was wonderful with individual clients, even group-therapy sessions, but he tended to clutch when it came to formal deliveries. It didn't surprise her that he'd waited until the last minute to prepare. It was a phenomenon called push-it-out-of-your-mind-until-you're-up-against-the-wall.

"I'll take the group," she said. She'd done it before. She never minded filling in for one of her partners, if only for the solace it gave her that they'd do the favor in return. Not that she'd ever had to ask. But someday she might. "It's at two?"

"You're free. I checked."

She made a note for herself, then eyed Peter without raising her head. "You're really nervous?"

"You could say that."

Propping her elbows on the desk, she smiled. "You'll do fine, Pete. Just sit down and plot out what you want to say. Make notes for yourself. You'll do fine."

"I'm supposed to speak for forty-five minutes, then open the floor for questions. Knowing my luck, there won't be any."

"Make a list of your own questions. If they're tongue-tied, you can get them going."

"I think I should take a course in public speaking."

He was probably right, but it was a little late for that now. "Just blot out the crowd and pretend that you're speaking with a small, cozy group."

"Easier said than done."

"It's mind over matter."

He shot her a crooked smile. "Where have I heard that before?"

They both thought of the cubby of a kitchen down the hall. Weeks ago, someone had taped that very message on the small refrigerator. Caroline guessed that it had been Maren, who was forever fighting the battle of the bulge. Then again, it could have been Norman, who was trying to cut down on canned sodas. Or Peter himself, who had an ice-cream habit he was trying to break. For that matter, she mused, the others could suspect her. Beside her supply of yogurt was a bag of bite-sized Almond Joys; choosing between the two was often a trial.

"Y'know," Caroline said, "it was probably Jason who put up that sign." Jason was a part-timer, their work-study secretary, and he teased them all mercilessly about their weaknesses. More than once she'd caught him with an Almond Joy, so she'd been able to tease him back. "Think he snitches your ice cream?"

"Let's just say that I found a paper cup with mocha remains in his wastebasket last week."

"You're into scavenging?"

That coaxed a chuckle from him. "Looking for the notes that I've never written for this speech." He drew himself up to his full five foot eight and headed for the door. "I'd better get to it. Thanks for this afternoon, Caroline. I appreciate it."

"No problem," she said sincerely. She'd simply write up her reports later.

With a glance at the small digital clock on her desk, she lifted the phone and punched out the number her mother had given her. As she'd suspected, neither of the doctors was available. She left a message and hung up the phone, then had just enough time to finish her yogurt and freshen up in the ladies' room before her one-o'clock appointment arrived.

That meeting went well, as did the group session at two. She'd conducted it before and knew the eight teenagers, all of whom were plagued by social insecurity. They accepted her as part of the therapy team, and after the first predictably slow fifteen minutes, things picked up.

She was pleased about that, particularly when her three-o'clock appointment turned out to be the pits. She'd been counseling Paul and Sheila Valente for five months. In their mid-thirties and married eight years, they'd developed communication problems that were putting a definite crimp in their relationship. They both worked full-time at high-pressure jobs, yet they managed to spare an hour a week to see her. She'd always seen that as a positive sign.

Suddenly Paul decided that they were wasting their time. "I don't see any progress," he announced the instant they were seated. Caroline was amazed he'd been able to wait even that long; she'd seen the thunder in his eyes when she first greeted him back in the waiting room and knew that the clouds had been gathering for some time. "Sheila goes to work. She comes home and thinks about work. Once in a while she remembers I'm there, but for the most part I could be a picture on the wall. If she's not willing to make an effort, no amount of counseling will help."

"I make an effort," Sheila argued, as eager to fight as he, "but each time I suggest we do something, either you have your own work to do or you want to work out or watch the baseball game."

"Those are things that I enjoy," he said, thumping his chest self-righteously. "There are plenty of other times when I'm doing absolutely nothing. That's when you choose to open your briefcase."

Sheila glared at the wall. "I see no reason why it always has to be me accommodating you, rather than the other way around." She turned her glare on Caroline. "I have to time my getting up in the morning so that the steam from my shower will have gone by the time he reaches the bathroom."

"That's not true. You need the extra time to fiddle with your makeup and try on three outfits before you finally decide what to wear."

"I have to look good at work. Clothes and makeup are important."

Sheila headed her own beauty-consulting service. Caroline had to admit that she always looked stunning. Not that Paul was a slouch. He was blond and good-looking, not overly tall but well built. He managed a large hotel not far from the Capitol, an enviable position for one so young.

"See?" Paul asked. "It's always work. When we finally manage to be free on the same evening, she doesn't want to go anywhere. She says that she dresses up every day and needs a break." He turned to his wife. "Well, I need a break, too. I need a wife who tries to please *me* for a change."

"You want to be doted on. Paul, that's passé. I'm not your mother. And do you dote on me?"

He snorted. "If I started, there'd be no end to it. Give you an inch and you'd take a mile. Look what happened with paying the bills. We agreed that we'd each take care of our own. Then one month you were too busy, so I gave you a hand. The month after that it was—" he affected a whiny soprano "—'You're so much better at it than I am, Paul,' so I did it again. Since then you've just assumed I'd do it."

"I work, damn it. I face bills day in, day out."

"Well, damn it," he yelled, throwing his hands in the air, "so do I!" He turned to Caroline. "She's obsessed with her role as the working woman. I didn't ask her to work. We don't need the income."

"We do if we want that house in Silver Spring."

"*You're* the one who wants it. I'd be just as happy to stay in the condo we have here and look for a house when we really need one. Like when we have kids. But that's a whole other can of worms. When we were first married, we said we'd wait two or three years before having children. Then you felt that the opportunity to consult at Bloomingdale's was too good to pass up, so we agreed to put off the kids a little longer. Then you started your own business—things were hot, you said, and you didn't want to lose your contacts—so it was shoved off again.

Why in the hell do we need a big house if we don't have a family to fill it?"

"A family's a moot point when we can't stand being near each other in bed."

"Speak for yourself. I reach for you and either your nails are still wet or you've just creamed your face or you have cramps—"

On and on they went, while Caroline listened silently. At last, she held up her hands to signal a cease-fire. "You're both angry, and that's okay. It's good that you can let go here. I only wish you could do it at home."

"He'd turn up the television."

"She'd lock herself in the bathroom."

Caroline raised a single hand this time. "I want you to sit back for a minute and think. You're both bottlers. We've talked about it before. You hold things in until you're ready to explode. It was my impression, though, that things had been getting a little better. I thought you were beginning to talk. Either I was mistaken or something happened this week to set you back."

"Nothing happened," Paul said. "*Nothing* happened. That's just the point. I want *something* to happen. I want a show of her feelings, one way or the other, but she says nothing."

Caroline looked at Sheila, inviting a response. What she got was a belligerent "Why do I have to take the first step?"

"Why not?" Paul countered. "I take the lead in just about everything else. I was the one who suggested we come here. I was the one to compromise when you said you wanted a woman therapist." He turned to Caroline. "But it's not working. She doesn't want therapy. I don't think she ever had any intention of changing. These sessions are pointless."

"That's the most intelligent deduction you've made in years," Sheila decided. With that, she rose from her seat and left the office.

Paul stared after her in disbelief, then shifted his disbelief to Caroline. "Why didn't you say something? You could have stopped her."

Caroline was disturbed herself, but she was trained not to show it. "Not if she wanted to leave. She knows how I feel about our sessions. She knows that I think they're helpful, even when they become free-for-alls."

"So what happens now?"

"We let her cool off."

"We?"

"You. You give her a little time. Tomorrow or the next day, you can broach the subject of coming back."

"Tomorrow or the next day—that's optimistic. When Sheila's angry, she can go for a week without acknowledging my presence."

"And you?" Caroline asked gently but pointedly.

He considered that for a minute, then shrugged.

"What set things off this time, Paul?"

He rubbed a hand across the back of his neck. "Who knows? We had the big guns visiting the hotel this week, so I spent three nights there working late. Each time, she was in bed when I got home, and she's never been a morning person." The hand kept rubbing. He looked legitimately tired.

"So you didn't have a chance to talk. How about this week? Will your schedule be as bad?"

"No."

"Why don't you make a date with her?"

"If she doesn't want to talk, she'll turn me down."

"You could try."

"I doubt it would work."

"What do you have to lose?"

He looked Caroline in the eye and said, "Pride."

She had to credit him with honesty. Pride didn't make her job any easier, but the client's recognition of it was a first step. "Well, then," she said, "what do you want to do?"

"About these sessions?"

She nodded.

He dropped his hand to the armrest. "If Sheila and I don't work something out, we might as well call it quits."

"Is that what you want?"

"Deep down, no. But I can't stand the way we are together. We share an apartment. That's about it. Once in a while we share meals. But fun? Laughter? I want a wife who's a friend. Right about now, I don't like Sheila very much."

"Right about now, you're angry and hurt."

"You're right. So what do I do?"

"Calm down. Wait for Sheila to do the same. Then talk. Quietly and sensibly. Tell her what you just told me. See what she says."

Caroline could see the argument forming on Paul's lips. He paused, clamped his lips together and finally nodded. When he stood to leave, she accompanied him to the door.

"If either of you wants to talk during the week, you have my number. Try to get her back here, Paul. Even if you decide to terminate, a final session would be wise. We've left too many things up in the air. If I can sum up a little, share my thoughts with you both, you'll be in a better position to decide what to do from there."

He nodded, thanked her, then left. Returning to her desk, Caroline sat quietly for a bit. As always happened at times like these, she reviewed the session, wondering what she might have done differently. Unfortunately, as always happened at times like these, her next client arrived before she'd reached any conclusions.

By the time that client, plus two others, had come and gone, it was six o'clock. Pushing aside mental exhaustion, she joined her partners for their regular Thursday-night meeting. At its conclusion, she returned to her office to find her sister-in-law, Diane, slouched in a chair.

"I need to talk."

"Oh, Di," Caroline whispered.

"He's impossible. I know he's your brother, but I'm your friend. I have no idea how to handle him."

"And I do?"

"If anybody does, it's you. You know where he's coming from, and besides, this is your specialty."

Caroline thought of the session with the Valentes and felt a heavy weight inside. She thought of the follow-up phone call she still had to put through to her father's doctors, and the one to her mother. She thought of the folders piled on the corner of her desk, waiting for the addition of notes from the day.

"Let's go for drinks," Diane suggested. "You look as discouraged as I feel."

At least she'd noticed, Caroline mused. There were times when she wondered whether anyone thought of her feelings. But Diane was a friend, a good friend. They went back a long way and she felt deeply for Diane's present turmoil.

"Okay," she said as she began to load the folders into a briefcase to take home. "A drink. Just one. I can't begin to tell you all I still have to do tonight."

IT WAS AFTER NINE when she finally reached the loft. She didn't begrudge the time she'd spent with Diane, because it had been productive. Over glasses of wine, they'd discussed Diane's resentment of Carl, who was having a tough time at work and had chosen to blame it on his marriage. Over chef's salads, they'd discussed the effect of the separation on Amy, who was four years old and devoted to both her parents. Over raspberry sherbet, they'd discussed the tug-of-war that the divorce settlement was becoming. And over lingering cups of coffee, they'd discussed the fact that, when all was said and done, Diane still loved her husband.

Caroline had every intention of telling that to Carl, but not tonight. Not tonight. There was too much else to do. She was bone tired and mentally saturated.

And hot. The loft was as bad as it had been the night before. As she'd done then, she flipped on the fan, opened the French windows, then stood in the semidarkness and played back the answering machine.

Her mother had called, bless her impatient soul. And Ben, no doubt checking to make sure she hadn't lied about late meetings. And one of her clients, who was sick and wanted to cancel her next day's leadoff appointment. Caroline didn't stop to wonder whether the sickness was real; she was too grateful to have the extra time to make up for the work that she suspected she might not get done tonight.

There was no return call from either of the doctors. She phoned their number and left her name as a reminder, then phoned her mother to relate the non-news. Dripping with sweat by this point, she peeled off her clothes, took a quick shower to wake herself up, pulled on a sleeveless nightshirt and, bending forward, secured her hair in a barrette at her crown. Then, pushing aside the small plant that was normally her centerpiece, she sat down at the round kitchen table with a low lamp, a tall glass of iced water and her briefcase.

Concentration didn't come easily. That morning seemed so far away that she had to struggle to recall the contents of those early sessions. Her mind wandered to the Valentes, to her parents, to Carl and Diane, while her eye wandered to the window.

His apartment was dark. She wondered whether he was out on a date or simply working late. Propping her chin on her palm, she closed her eyes and pictured herself out with him. They wouldn't go to the symphony, or the theater, or a movie. They'd go to an intimate restaurant where the ambience would more than make up for the lack of conversation. Even without that ambience, they wouldn't have to talk. He'd understand her exhaustion. He'd know that it was the quiet companionship that mattered.

Opening her eyes with some effort, she trained them on the folder marked Meecham, Nicole. She squared a pad of paper before her, lifted her pen and began to write. *Client initiated discussion of her superior at work. She resents what she sees as condescension on his part, and this fuels the anger she feels toward her parents. Independence is becoming a central issue in therapy, as is self-worth.*

She dropped the pen and took a cool drink. Independence. In some ways she'd always been independent, in others never. What was independence, anyway? Was it a state of mind or a physical state? And self-worth? Oh, she had a sense of that, all right. The people in her world wouldn't let her forget that she was their mainstay. She wished they would, once in a while. There were times when she wanted to lean on someone else.

What she needed, she decided, dropping her head back with a tired sigh, was a vacation. Not the kind she usually took—visiting her parents and her sister—but a real, honest-to-goodness vacation. A remote spot. No telephone. No responsibility. Total anonymity.

Well, almost total. Her gaze crept out the window and across the courtyard. She'd take a vacation with him. He'd pick the spot, a sparsely populated island in the Caribbean. . . . No, no, a remote cabin in northernmost Maine, where the nights were blessedly cool. He'd drive her there in his Jaguar. It'd be a long drive, but she'd sleep most of the way. She wouldn't have to keep an eagle's eye on the road as she did with Elliot, who, she was convinced, had done his driver training at Macy's. Tall-Dark-and-Handsome would be a careful driver. She'd be able to relax and rest.

Without conscious thought, she rose from the table and went to the window. Tucking one leg beneath her, she perched on the end of the seat with her arms wrapped around her waist and her shoulder braced against the frame.

He'd wake her when they reached their remote cabin, but he'd do it gently, and the first thing he'd do after he unlocked the door would be to pull back the sheets of the bed. They'd be crisp cotton sheets, smelling of the fresh outdoors in a way no dryer could simulate. She'd stretch out and soon be asleep, but when she awoke in the morning, he'd be with her.

And then . . . And then they'd make long, sweet, passionate love.

She drew in a wispy breath at the thought, then held that breath in her lungs when the light in his apartment came on. His window was already wide open. Either he'd been home earlier or he was more trusting than she.

Whatever the case, she could easily follow his movements, which she did with more fascination than guilt.

He wore a body-molding tank top, a pair of running shorts and sneakers, and his skin glistened with sweat. He was tall indeed, she discovered with pleasure. His head well exceeded the top of the refrigerator, from which he was taking a drink. His back muscles flexed with the action; they weren't at all bunchy but were nicely formed and well toned. As he straightened, held the can to his mouth and tipped his head back for a drink, she saw that his shoulders were broad without being inflated and his torso tapered to wonderfully narrow hips.

The tingles were off and running. She was a little appalled, because she'd never been one to sit ogling men. But those tingles felt so good and healthy that she gave them free rein. More than that, she encouraged them as she mentally transferred the body in her sights to that cabin in Maine...to that bed...to that exquisitely gentle but fiercely satisfying lovemaking.

When Tall-Dark-and-Handsome turned toward the window, she held her breath. She knew she should move away, but she couldn't. The best she could do was avert her eyes for a minute, but, with a will of its own, that gaze quickly returned to watch while he flipped a newspaper open on the table and stood reading.

The *Wall Street Journal*. She couldn't possibly see, of course, but she knew it was that. No stuffy journals dealing with medicine or education or psychology for him. He'd be one to broaden himself.

But she didn't really want to think of his mind at the moment, when his body was hers for the looking. Gorgeous. That was all there was to it. He was gorgeous. His hair wasn't as long as she'd hoped, but it was well mussed and clearly sweaty. His chin—only one, not even a hint of a double—was tucked neatly to his chest, which was hugged so snugly by his tank top that she wondered at its purpose. It had to be to absorb sweat, she decided, because if he'd worn it for propriety's sake, he'd failed. There was nothing remotely proper about the way he looked in the thing, or the way it met his low-riding shorts . . . or the way those shorts cupped his sex.

When a shiver coursed from her shoulders to her knees, she wondered if she'd gone too far. Shivers—in the heat? But, oh, Lord, he was combing a handful of fingers through his hair now, and the way he raised his arm, the shadow beneath, the delineation of his collar-bone, the prominent veins on the inside of his fore-arm—more shivers, delicious ones, frustrating ones.

Tearing herself from the window, she made a beeline for the table, sat back down and clutched her pen. Only after the fact did it occur to her that she should have been more subtle. If the abrupt movement had attracted his attention, he'd be watching her now. She cast a glance at the lamp. To turn it off would defeat her purpose; she really had to work. It didn't light much of the room, which had suited her fine in terms of the heat, but it did light *her*, and if he was looking across the courtyard as she'd been doing seconds before, he'd have a clear view.

Donning an expression of intense concentration, she began to write. *Client is deeply into fantasizing. It's a rather new experience for her. Either she's been too busy to do it before or she didn't have the need. I suspect that it's a combination of both. Then again, she may have re-pressed the need. Or she may feel herself above it. Counselors do that sometimes.*

Slowly setting down the pen, she carefully tore the sheet of paper from its pad, folded it in half, then in quarters, and tucked it into the space between the small clay pot that held her creeping Charlie and the slightly larger and more brightly colored pot in which the clay one sat.

With that touch of self-analysis out of the way, she settled down to work in earnest. Discipline had always been her strong suit, and she called on it now to guide her through the reports that she wanted to have done by morning. From time to time she paused for a drink, or to brush dots of moisture from her nose, or to massage the muscles of her lower back.

By eleven, she was ready for a break. Unfolding herself from the chair, she arched her back and stretched, then raised both hands to the top of her head. When the phone rang, she slowly looked its way.

Not exactly the break she had in mind, but beggars couldn't be choosers.

"Hello?"

"I didn't wake you, did I?"

"Of course not. What's wrong, Elliot?" The flatness of his voice, an about-face from the night before, was a dead giveaway.

"Celebration's over. Did I say that this developer would be tough to work with? Make that impossible. We spent the whole day arguing with him about the architect's specs. They're absurd. Half of the stuff he's got listed can't be bought."

"Why did the architect list them?"

"Because he's an arrogant S.O.B. who did his training in Milan. Well, hell, we can't go to Milan for materials. Not if we want to make any profit on this thing."

"The developer must know that."

"Sure he knows it. But he doesn't give a damn about our profit. He's out for himself."

"Oh, Elliot, there must be some way to make him understand," she said. Grabbing a nearby dish towel, she began to dust the peninsula on which the phone sat. When Elliot said nothing, she remarked, "At least you have partners to argue on your side. It's not your responsibility alone."

"That's the problem," Elliot said in a quiet voice.

"What is?"

"I was the one who came up with the bid on these particular specs."

"You bid on the wrong materials?" She couldn't believe he'd do something so stupid. Then again, he'd been desperate to land the job.

"I bid on materials that I felt were of equivalent quality. The developer knew what I'd priced, but now he's decided that he wants the originals."

"Can you charge him for the difference?"

"Not with the contract already signed."

"So what will you do?"

"Either absorb the difference or fight."

Caroline's hand stilled on the cloth. She didn't feel like dusting. It was too hot. She sighed. "I guess you have a decision to make, then."

"I'm damned either way. On top of that, we found out today that we'll have to do a whole lot of blasting if we want to put in an underground parking lot."

"You didn't know that before?" she asked. By the time he'd launched into a long story about topographical charts, she was seeking diversions. While she'd never found Elliot's trials and tribulations fascinating, they'd been interesting enough. It was his petulant tone that put her off now. That and the heat.

She ought to get a small air conditioner, she decided. But where to put it? She couldn't set it in one of the French windows; that would ruin their look, not to mention the luxury of being able to open both wide. The only other window was in the bathroom, so a window unit was out. She could have one installed in the wall, but that would take major construction, which she doubted her landlords would condone.

Hell, she didn't want an air conditioner. She wanted a magic carpet.

"It'll probably be awful," Elliot was saying. "So give me something to look forward to. I can pick you up at work and we'll do something wild."

"When?"

"Tomorrow night."

"But we have plans for Saturday."

"We can do something tomorrow, too."

Shifting the phone to the other ear, she rubbed her stiff shoulder and leaned back against the counter. "I can't, Elliot. I'm so far behind with paperwork that I'll be late at the office."

"Name a time and I'll come."

"If I don't get my work done, I'll have to spend part of Saturday at it, and I've already got a list a mile long of things to do for Saturday."

"I need you, Caroline."

It was a cheap shot. He was playing on her softness, and actually, she couldn't blame him. It usually worked. But not tonight. She was tired of being a doormat. "Elliot, I can't. Really. Saturday night has your name on it in big red letters."

"If I didn't know better, I'd think you were two-timing me."

"With work?" she asked. Her eye crossed the courtyard.

"With a man. Are you seeing someone else?"

Tall-Dark-and-Handsome moved through her line of vision. She couldn't see what he was doing, because he was fast moving out of sight, but a hunter-green towel was draped around his neck. He must have been wiping off sweat.

She gave a helpless little moan. At its sound, she bit her lip, then realized that it wasn't so bad; the moan could be taken two ways. "I don't have time to see two men," she answered, realizing only after the fact that her words could be taken two ways, too.

Elliot took both moan and words to his benefit. "Good. I'm feeling possessive."

She was careful to stifle the moan this time. "When should I expect you Saturday?"

"I'll give you a call during the day."

"Better tell me now," she warned in as teasing a tone as she could muster. "I'll be running all day, and I don't want you to have to talk to the machine."

"Okay. How does six-thirty sound?"

"Fine, Elliot. See you then."

She hung up the phone and slowly turned to face the window. As slowly, she began to walk, stopping only when her thighs touched the window seat. Lowering herself to her customary position against the jamb, she wrapped her arms around her legs and looked over the cars and trees to the opposite loft.

From what she could see, it was set up almost identically to hers. The living area was in the foreground. Beyond it and taking up most of the wall to the left of the front door was the kitchen. To the right of the door was the sleeping area.

The similarities to her own place ended there. His furniture was of a soft brown leather and distinctly masculine, while hers was upholstered in a bright floral print that favored pale greens and pinks. His kitchen table was square and lacquered in a dark shade of tan with chairs of leather and chrome, while her table was round and its chairs of matching light birch. And while her bed was a double and wore a quilt to match her sofa, his was king-sized and covered with . . . covered with . . . a jumble of sheets.

She smiled. He was a slob. His bed wasn't the only thing in a state of disarray. Mail littered the peninsula by the door. Magazines and newspapers were strewn on the coffee table in the living area. A suit jacket, replete with tie, had been left draped over the leather side chair. And she swore she could see the very tip of a pile of dishes in the sink.

If he thought she was going to clean up after him, he had another thing coming. Still, there was something appealing about his mess. It suggested that he was laid-back, and she liked that. Ben had been a compulsive cleaner, and the compulsiveness had carried over into other aspects of his life. He'd been ultraorganized, both at work and at home, and punctual to the extreme of sitting in his car until the stroke of eight, if that was the time they were to meet another couple for dinner.

Tall-Dark-and-Handsome wasn't hung up that way. He didn't stand on ceremony. He was spontaneous and took enjoyment from the sheer act of living. She decided that his apartment looked more lived-in than messy and she liked that, too.

Just then, the object of her speculation came into view. She clutched her knees tighter against the impulse to hide from sight, for she couldn't do that. It was too late. He'd come to lean against the window and was looking straight at her.

Her toes curled. She began to tingle. A knot of excitement formed in her chest and worked its way to her throat, making each breath an effort.

Gone were the tank top and running shorts. The towel that had earlier been draped around his neck now swathed his hips. He'd come from the shower. She didn't ask herself how she knew that the moisture on his skin wasn't sweat. She couldn't possibly tell the difference from where she sat. But she knew.

His body shone. For a fleeting second she imagined that it was wreathed by a halo, but she caught herself on that particular bit of fantasy. He wasn't a saint. Lord, she didn't *want* a saint. She wanted a man, just a man, sweet idiosyncrasies and all.

He didn't nod his head or lift a hand. There was no movement except the slow, barely perceptible rise and fall of his chest.

Sweat trickled down her cheek to her jaw. Her skin grew warmer, this time from within. She had the split-second vision of her body sparking, then disintegrating into a little puff of smoke. Before the vision had passed, she knew she had to move.

Turning her head first, she very carefully pushed herself from the seat. As calmly, she crossed to the kitchen table, neatly returned her papers to the briefcase, then switched off the light. Knowing that he could no longer see, she gave vent to the tiny tremors in her limbs and less steadily pulled back the quilt on her bed and stretched out atop the smooth sheets.

She didn't look back at the window. Her head was turned away, eyes closed. But the last images to register behind those lids before she fell asleep were of a cool cascade of water, a bar of Irish Spring and a hunter-green towel lying discarded on the floor.

# 3

BRENDAN CARR was bewitched. That was the only conclusion he could reach when at the oddest moments of
the day his thoughts turned to Sweet-and-Sexy. He'd
come to think of her as that. The name fit. There was a
sweetness to her—in the lyrical way she moved her
hands, the girlish way she gathered her hair into a
ponytail, the graceful way she roamed her apartment.
He might have called her innocent, for he imagined he
saw that, too, but sexiness overrode it.

Was she ever sexy! The thin bits of cloth she wore in
the heat hid everything essential while hiding nothing at
all. She was slender without being skinny. He knew that
her breasts were small but well rounded, that her waist
was narrow, that her hips flared just enough to flaunt her
femininity. She didn't flaunt it knowingly; he was convinced of that. She couldn't see the way the dim back-
light of her loft passed through material to outline her
curves. He sensed that she'd be embarrassed if she knew,
or maybe that was what he wanted to believe. He wanted
to believe many things. Hell, what man wouldn't, when
a woman turned him on the way she did?

He wanted to believe, first off, that she was single. She
lived alone, but that didn't mean that she wasn't separated from a husband or engaged to another man or bid-
ing her time until the object of her true love returned
from a faraway place. He'd seen a man in her apartment
several times, and though she'd kissed him goodbye

when he'd left, she'd deliberately freed herself from his embrace before it had escalated. They'd certainly never made it to the bed.

With the march of those words through his mind, he grimaced. He wasn't really a Peeping Tom. But the French windows were huge in relation to the loft, and he was only human. At night, with the lights on, little was hidden. She hadn't covered the windows with drapes, apparently seeing the travesty of that, a woman of his own mind.

Actually, he'd been acutely aware of that loft since he'd moved into his own two years before. Its previous tenants had been a pair of coeds who had partied nonstop. Even in the dead of winter—though Washington's winters were far from frigid—they'd had no compunction about throwing the windows open wide to share their raucous gatherings with the world. The noise had been horrendous. He hadn't been the only tenant annoyed, but he'd been one of the few who'd dared speak up. Toward the end of their stay, the two girls had taken to tossing derogatory cracks across the courtyard at him. He'd been relieved when they'd moved out.

That had been six months ago. Naturally, he'd been curious about the new tenant. He'd assumed that the realty firm—the same one that owned the entire block of town houses—had been more careful this time, particularly since they'd been left with a monumental cleaning and painting job. The winter months had been quiet and he'd been busy, but when the first of the good weather had rolled around, he'd cast an occasional curious glance across the way.

He'd never forget the night he'd first seen her. He'd been scanning the front page of the *Journal* when the sudden illumination of her apartment had caught his eye.

Unable to resist, he'd leaned back against the counter and watched over the top of the paper.

She'd just come in from work. At least, he'd assumed that was it, since she was dressed more smartly and seemed older—strike that, more mature—than a student. She'd shrugged out of her blazer and laid it on the bed, then transferred a frozen dinner from the freezer to the microwave.

He remembered feeling badly that she was eating alone, then wondering why he should. She was attractive. If she'd wanted a dinner partner, she could have found one.

So he'd thrust aside any feelings of guilt and gone back to his paper that night, but he hadn't been able to keep his eye from wandering on other nights.

You could learn a lot about a woman by spying, he mused. You could learn, for example, that she was dedicated to her work, if the long hours she kept and the homework she did were any indication. And that she was a creature of habit—entering her apartment each night, flipping on the light, placing the mail on the counter, opening the French windows, weather permitting, and turning on the answering machine, in that order. And that she was neat—unless she had a daily maid who cleaned up after her. He couldn't possibly know about that, since he was at work himself and, anyway, couldn't see into her loft in broad daylight. But when she came home at night, the place was always tidy. Of course, in contrast to his own place, anything would seem tidy.

Over the weeks, he'd come to think about her more and more. Somehow, returning to his apartment hadn't seemed quite as lonely when he could look forward to a glimpse of her. For the longest time she'd been unaware of him, and he'd had mixed feelings about that. On the one hand, he'd wanted to be able to wave or smile or call across the courtyard to her. On the other hand, he'd been satisfied to set reality aside and simply dream.

He'd done a lot of that. He dreamed that she was his ideal, and though he'd never spent a great deal of time formulating ideals, she embodied them all. She had a career but wasn't an ardent feminist, never letting her job take precedence over the personal life she wanted. And she did want a personal life, he dreamed. She simply hadn't found the proper channel.

He dreamed that she was warm and giving, a dream abetted by the amount of time she spent on the phone. He knew that they weren't frivolous, chatty little calls, because she'd often rub her neck or hang her head. The calls frustrated her, but still she took them. She was a selfless sort.

And a loaner. More than once she'd answered her door to find one of the neighbors in search of something— butter, sugar, eggs. Usually it was Connie. He knew Connie. He bumped into her on and off by their cars in the courtyard and found her to be a little too aggressive for his tastes. And too old. He was thirty-eight. Though Connie was a looker, she was over forty if she was a day. Perhaps it was a hang-up of his, but he wanted a younger woman—not a teenybopper, simply one who hadn't been around quite so much.

Sweet-and-Sexy looked to be in her late twenties, which was just about right, as far as he was concerned. The nine- or ten-year advantage meant that he was well established at work and could provide for her as he saw fit.

If she was in her late twenties, she'd have completed her education and had time to put down roots in a career. Money wasn't the issue; it was more one of self-respect. Her self-respect. The stronger an image she had of herself as a person, the more comfortable she'd be with herself as a woman.

And she was comfortable. He could see it in the unselfconscious way she dressed and moved. Actually, sexy was the wrong word, because it implied that she was aware of the effect. Sensual was more apt, but Sweet-and-Sensual didn't roll as well off his tongue, and sexy was what she made him feel.

Particularly over these past few days of intense heat. When he was home he wore shorts and little else. It wasn't that his own bareness turned him on, but feeling half-naked as he watched her floating in whisper-thin shifts was phenomenally erotic. As was sweat.

He'd always known he had an earthy side, but it had never before emerged as strongly. He loved the way she looked when she was hot, when her skin was flushed and silky tendrils of hair clung to her neck. He didn't want a woman who perspired daintily. He wanted a woman who produced real, honest-to-goodness sweat, like he did. And he wanted a woman who reacted to it like she did—gracefully wiping her brow with the back of her hand, arching her spine in a catlike stretch, tipping her head to place a tall, cooling glass against her neck, slanting against the window in an unconsciously sultry pose.

Then, two nights ago, she'd looked up and seen him. Fantasy and reality had suddenly blurred, which was ridiculous, since he didn't really know anything more about her than he'd known before. But there had been something about the way she'd looked at him—as though she was a little shocked, a little fascinated, more than a little unsure of what to do about either—that focused things a bit more.

Was it time to act? He'd asked himself that question dozens of times in the past two days. He wanted to make that first verbal contact, but somehow that would bring reality even closer, and he wasn't sure if he was ready. His hesitance seemed silly, when he thought about it, because he'd never been diffident or shy. He attributed it to the fantasy, which was so lovely that he didn't want it to end.

Of course, if reality were to prove even better, he'd curse himself for the waste of time. She was so pretty, so sensual, so gentle looking. He could imagine himself relaxing with her, and he badly needed to relax. He could imagine the soft conversations they'd have and those times when they wouldn't even have to talk, feeling perfectly comfortable sharing the silence.

He could also imagine her in bed. Not just *in* bed. He'd caught glimpses of her there moments before she'd turned off her light. It was enchanting the way she'd stretched out, curved around, found a pleasant spot beneath the sheet. But that wasn't what he'd had in mind. He could imagine her in bed *with him*, offering the deepest softness and the sweetest fire.

"Hey, Brendan. We've got a problem."

His head came up and he straightened in his chair, but only the long finger he used to brush sweat from above his lip suggested that his mind had been on anything but work.

His underling seemed not to have noticed, but then, Kevin Brauer had never been particularly observant. He wouldn't notice a man sweating in an air-conditioned room any more than he'd notice the black ink on a counterfeiter's thumb. He was a technician, good for researching, chasing down leads and setting up schedules—the last of which, Brendan assumed correctly, was what had brought him around with such an aggrieved expression on his face.

"Smith doesn't want to testify."

Brendan flexed his sore racquetball shoulder. "That's nothing new. He's said so before."

"But he's refusing to show for the hearing. He says that he has to fly to Dallas on business and won't be back until next Wednesday. If the hearing's set for Tuesday—"

"He'll have to change his plans. We've already postponed things twice to accommodate him. Accommodating time's over."

"What should I tell him?"

The set of Brendan's jaw hinted at impatience directed more toward Kevin than Harold Smith. "Just what I said. Accommodating time's over."

"And if he balks?"

"Subpoena him."

"Subpoena," Kevin echoed with a vigorous nod as he withdrew his head from the door. "Right."

Brendan let out a mocking snort and wondered about the Kevins of the world. They were, by and large, bright and had graduated law school with honors. But the regurgitation of book facts was one thing; creative thinking was another. Lawyers like Kevin were misplaced in the criminal division, where instincts were crucial. They'd do far better in antitrust or civil or tax.

But the Kevins of the world specifically wanted criminal. They envisioned high intrigue and action. Little did they know that the highest intrigue at this level of law enforcement was strictly intellectual and that the heart of the action was a war of wills.

Kevin Brauer did not have the personality to win a war of wills. Brendan did. A patient man, he spent a lot of time thinking, just thinking, mulling over the scores of

documents he read each month, trying to identify pat-
terns and anticipate moves. It was puzzle solving at its
best, a battle of wits. Given his natural curiosity, the
ability to project himself into other worlds and minds,
an intricate knowledge of the law, an uncanny sense of
timing and staunch determination, he had the edge.

The Smith case was a perfect example. Harold Smith
owned a chemical plant similar in size and structure to
two others that had been threatened with sabotage in the
past year. Brendan's instinct, aided by voluminous re-
search and an unconfirmed source, told him that Smith's
plant was next in line. Though they all knew that the
threat of chemical contamination of food sources or water supplies was a lethal weapon in the hands of terrorists, Harold Smith was resisting. He downplayed the
vulnerability of his plant and the possibility that one of
his employees was on the take. He didn't want adverse
publicity to result from an investigation that he believed
would go nowhere.

Brendan's job now was to quietly but firmly convince
him that the publicity would be that much more adverse
if he failed to cooperate.

His intercom beeped, jarring him from his thoughts.
He jabbed at the button on the speaker phone. "Yes,
Marge?"

"Miss Wills on line four. Are you in?"

He wished he weren't, but he'd already put off the persistent Miss Wills twice today. "I'm in," he said with a
sigh, then switched off the speaker, pressed line four and
lifted the receiver. "Hi, Jocelyn."

"Does Marge hate me?" came the soft female voice.

Brendan had to smile. "Of course not."

"I think I annoy her when I call."

"Only because when I'm not here she has to make excuses, and too often I'm not here."

"I keep missing you," Jocelyn said with such genuine sadness that Brendan felt more than a twinge of guilt. Jocelyn Wills was a very lovely woman whom he'd dated on and off in the past few months. He liked her, but that was all, and when he'd sensed that her feelings had grown deeper than his, he'd tried to cool it.

Jocelyn wasn't taking the hint. With the license granted the modern woman, she called him often. She even showed up at his apartment, "just to say hello." He wouldn't have minded the impromptu visits if it wasn't for the fact that, when she put him on the spot that way, he felt like a heel if he didn't ask her out. Inevitably he did. Inevitably he felt worse afterward. He knew that he should be more honest about his feelings, but he couldn't hurt her. She was sweet and innocuous. She'd been living in the capital less than a year. Her circle of friends was small. She was lonely.

But when she said things like "I keep missing you," the best he could do was play dumb to the double entendre.

"Things have been hectic here. We're trying to tie up all sorts of loose ends before people start taking off for summer vacations."

"Have you made your own plans yet?"

He squeezed his eyes shut and made a good-going-Brendan-you-jerk face. "Not yet, Jocelyn. I'm still waiting to see what the others plan to do."

"Why? You have seniority over most of them. Tell them when you're going away and let them plan around you."

"It doesn't work that way. With seniority comes greater responsibility. Besides, I can be more flexible than those who are trying to coordinate plans with their spouses and kids."

When Jocelyn didn't answer immediately, he knew precisely what she was thinking. She'd invited him to spend the last week of July with her at her family's place on Martha's Vineyard, and he'd been putting her off as tactfully as he could. No doubt she was hurt to have to play twentieth fiddle to his colleagues.

"I have to let my family know whether we want the house. My sister wants it the same week."

"Let her have it," Brendan said as gently as he could. "I honestly don't think I'll be able to get away for more than long weekends here and there."

"But you need the time off. When was your last vacation?"

"March."

"That doesn't count. You went to a conference."

He didn't bother to say that he'd taken several days for himself when the conference was through. He hadn't felt he'd been dating Jocelyn long enough to merit a joint vacation, or so he'd told himself at the time, but even back then he must have known that his feelings for her were finite. He wasn't a prude. If he'd wanted her, he'd have had her join him in a minute. But as pleasant as she was, she didn't excite him.

On the other hand, he could seriously consider kidnapping Sweet-and-Sexy and whisking her off for a month. Martha's Vineyard, Bar Harbor, Hilton Head . . . hell, he could take a suite at the nearest Marriott and be happy.

"Well," he said with a sigh that had nothing to do with vacation schedules, "conference or no, I was out of the office, so it was a break."

"I was looking forward to the Vineyard."

"Why don't you go anyway? The place is swarming with people in the summer."

"I was looking forward to going with you."

"I can't make it, Jocelyn."

"I'll hold the house for the week," she said with sudden resolve. "My sister will just have to make other plans."

"That's not fair."

"I'm tired of being fair. If I have the house, maybe you'll join me, even for a day or two."

"Jocelyn—"

"Don't say a word. Just know that the invitation is still open, okay?"

"It's not okay," he said in frustration. "Listen to me. If I take time off this summer, I'll be going off where no one can reach me. I'll want to be alone, isolated from everything to do with my life here."

"Isolated from me?" she asked in a small voice.

"Isolated from everyone."

"Oh." She thought about that for a while; then, for whatever her reasons, she decided against arguing. "Okay. But you'll still be welcome at the Vineyard during that last week in July." She took a quick breath. "But the real reason I'm calling is that there's going to be a lecture on Soviet-American relations next Thursday night at school. The Soviet ambassador will probably be there. I was planning on going and thought you might like to join me."

"Thursday night?" he echoed, buying time to decide what to do.

"At eight. Will you be busy that night?"

There was busy and there was busy. A quick glance at his desk calendar told him that he didn't have anything formal on the agenda. But if he didn't have work to do at home, he might want to play raquetball or read a good book...or sit in his darkened apartment and stare across the courtyard.

"Uh..."

"If you have plans, I'll understand."

If only she *wouldn't* understand. When she spoke so gently and sincerely, he felt badly all over again. "No, I don't have plans."

"Would you like to go?"

Soviet-American relations? Hell, the topic was good. He always enjoyed hearing a new slant. "Sure, Jocelyn. Should I meet you there?" She worked at American, which was how she came to be on the inside track for the university's lectures.

"Unless you want to catch a bite to eat beforehand," she suggested hopefully.

It occurred to him that that sounded too much like a date, while the beauty of meeting her at a lecture was its impersonality. He doubted she'd be any more attuned to the subtlety now than she'd been in the past, but he had to give it a try.

"Better let me get as much done here as I can. That way I won't feel as guilty about taking time for the lecture."

"Guilt will be your downfall, Brendan," she teased.

*You should only know*, he thought, but rather than follow up on her jibe, he simply asked her in what room the lecture was being held, promised to meet her there at eight and signed off.

THAT NIGHT, Brendan sat in his living room taking a good, long look at himself and his life. Sweet-and-Sexy's apartment was dark, but his self-examination had less to do with that fact and the possibility that he was bored than it had to do with the fantasy itself.

It frightened him a little, the depth of that fantasy. He'd always been more a doer than a dreamer. He'd always been active and busy, and he was now, but still he was dwelling on a fantasy that could prove as insubstantial as a wet tissue. He wondered why he was doing it. Was the void in his life that great?

He supposed, when he thought about it, that he was lonely. He was surrounded by people all day and by rights should be thrilled to spend his nights alone, and for the longest time that had been okay. Now, though, it seemed wrong. He wasn't sure when the change had taken place. Life had a way of speeding by, a blurred panorama of events that came into focus only when one slowed down to make a turn. He hadn't planned on turning. His subconscious must have stuck a hand on the wheel.

He wondered if it had something to do with his age. Women weren't the only ones aware of biological clocks. Any man who was active in sports knew that at thirty he was a tad slower than he'd been at twenty, at thirty-eight a tad slower than he'd been five years before. Brendan had never been bothered by that; what little he'd lost in speed he'd gained in finesse.

Nor was he vain; he didn't fear going gray or needing glasses or getting wrinkles. It was more a matter of health and strength. He wanted to be able to enjoy a wife and kids when he was in his prime, which brought him back to the biological clock. He was reaching his prime damn fast.

Sprawling lower on the sofa, he steepled his fingers against his mouth. Where *was* she? Her apartment was still dark as pitch, and it was nine o'clock. The thought of her on a date made him jealous. The thought of her away for the weekend left him in despair. Feeling distinctly antsy, he bolted from the chair and stalked into the bathroom. A tepid shower brought relief from the night's heat, but it did little to settle his mind. Moments later, barely dry, he tugged on a pair of nylon running shorts, grabbed a Miller Lite from the fridge and climbed onto the fire escape. Popping the tab with his thumb, he chugged a third of the can before setting it down on his knee.

He'd be a good catch, he argued in his own defense. He was easy to look at, easy to be with. Having lived alone for so long, he was self-sufficient. Okay, so his apartment wouldn't pass a white-glove test, but he knew the rudiments of cooking, regularly emptied the trash and, when inspiration struck, could make his bed. He came from good stock, had a solid education, a stable job in a stable profession. Granted, as a public servant he didn't earn the big bucks that he might in the private sector, but he had lived modestly over the years and had saved. If she gave the word, he'd buy a house. He kind of liked that idea. Something out of the city. Something with lots of privacy. Something with acres of land for the kids.

She'd want kids; he knew she would. She'd even want to put her job on hold while the kids were young. He'd never ask her to do it. It would be her own decision, but it would please him. He was a modern male and all, and he'd insist on doing his share when he was home. Still, that old-fashioned part of him believed kids did best in those early years when they were with their moms, particularly with moms like her.

He took another drink, then stared grimly into the dark. So he was into the fantasy again, and the scariest part was that it seemed so real and so right picturing Sweet-and-Sexy in his future.

*My man, you're in for a fall,* he told himself. *She'll turn out to be an accountant with a squeaky voice and an aversion to sex.*

But all such thoughts flew from his head then, because the light in her apartment came on. Teeth against his upper lip, he watched closely while she set the mail on the counter, laid down the blazer she'd been carrying along with her briefcase, opened the French windows wide, then turned on the answering machine. As she listened, she was working at freeing the buttons of her blouse. His teeth sank deeper when the blouse flared open, and though she kept her back to him, his imagination went wild.

That was all she allowed. Skirting the bed, she passed from his line of vision.

He was aching for more, his entire body tight. Exhaling the breath he'd held, he slowly drew in another, let it out, drew in another, let it out. By the time he'd gained a modicum of self-control, she was returning to the answering machine, wearing a very large, very long, pale-yellow T-shirt. No sooner had she switched off the machine than she walked to the window.

He held his ground. His pulse quickened, but he didn't look away.

Her shoulders were straight. Her arms hung gently by her sides. Though her face was in shadow, he knew the instant their eyes met. He felt it viscerally, that silent hello, and, counting on the force of brain waves, sent back his own.

*How was your day?* he asked.

*Better now,* she answered. *And yours?*

*Likewise. Is your apartment very hot?*

She trailed the flat of her hand down her neck. *Yes. But I don't mind. Air conditioners are noisy.*

*There wouldn't be anyplace to put one here. It'd be a shame to block the windows.*

*I agree.*

*You have a ceiling fan, don't you? I can't quite see.*

Her fingers crept up her scalp, drawing the weight of her hair from her neck. *I do.*

*I'm glad. It helps, doesn't it?*

*Yes.*

*Why don't you get something to drink? I feel guilty sitting here with my beer.*

*In a minute.* Her hand fell from her hair and came to rest lightly on her stomach. *I don't want to move just yet.*

But she did move, casting an abrupt glance over her shoulder. Only when he'd pulled himself from the fantasy did he hear a faint jangle. She looked back at him.

*It's the phone. Will you excuse me for a minute?*

*Sure.*

*You won't leave?*

*Nope.*

He imagined he saw the faintest smile curve her lips before she turned and trotted to the phone.


"FINALLY!"

Caroline's heart skipped a beat. "Karen? Is it the baby?"

"No. It's you! You're finally home! I tried you twice last night and then once earlier tonight."

That explained the clicks on her answering machine. "Why didn't you leave a message?"

"Because it didn't work last time. You didn't return my call."

Caroline felt duly chastised. "I was planning to call this weekend, when I had time to sit and really talk."

"Can you talk now?"

Could she talk with her sister? Of course she could. *I mean, enough is enough. When it gets to the point that you're imagining conversations with a man you've never met . . .*

Arcing an apologetic glance toward the window, she drew out one of the kitchen chairs and sank down. "Sure, Karen. I'd love to talk. Tell me how you're feeling."

"Fat and heavy and hot."

"That great?"

"Yeah."

"How's baby?"

Karen's voice picked up. "Kicking up a storm. Really hardy, says the doctor."

"That must make you feel good," Caroline returned with a smile. "I wish I could see."

"None of us can see."

"I mean touch."

"Everybody touches. It's weird, Caro. Everybody touches. I mean, it's my body, but everybody touches. *You* can touch. That's okay. Obviously *Dan* can, and my friends, even the people I work with every day. But clients?"

Caroline heard the tension in her sister's high-pitched babble. "They're envious," she said, but the soothing words were far more than mere platitude. She knew what she was saying. She felt that envy herself. "You have something they want."

"I try to remember that when my back aches and my ankles swell to twice their normal size."

"Twice?" Caroline chided.

"Well, maybe not twice, but close."

"That's normal, Karen. So are the backaches. Maybe you ought to take it a little easier."

"With work?"

"Mmm."

"I wish I could. But I'm just an associate."

"You're a *pregnant* associate."

"And the big boys are watching me closely. I'll be up for a partnership in a year. If I can't show them that I'm serious about my career, I can kiss that partnership goodbye."

"What does Dan say?" Dan was Karen's husband, and a nicer man Caroline couldn't have chosen for her sister. "He wouldn't care if the partnership was deferred, would he?"

"He wouldn't, but I would. I've worked so hard for this, Caro. To come so far and either have it postponed or lose it completely would break my heart."

"But you do want the baby."

"Yes, I want the baby. I want the baby and Dan *and* the partnership. I can do it, Caro. I know I can."

"So do I, but that doesn't mean it will be easy."

"Nothing's easy for a woman—especially in law. You wouldn't believe the discrimination that still exists."

"You've managed to handle it up to now," Caroline said by way of encouragement.

"But it's a constant fight. I think that's what discourages me most. In the best of circumstances I have to be twice as good as any man on my level, and now, with this pregnancy, I have to be *three* times as good. You'd think I had a terminal illness, the way the partners try to hide me from clients. I can understand in a way; a client doesn't want to come to rely on a lawyer who will be disappearing for a couple of months. But that's all it's going to be. Ninety days. The firm knows that. Ninety days!"

"Shh, Karen. It's okay."

"I'd really like to believe that. I have my moments of insecurity, too. Times when I think of what might happen if the baby is a screamer, or there's some physical problem—"

"The baby won't be a screamer," Caroline interrupted, "and there won't be a physical problem. Don't be like Mom, Karen. It's self-defeating."

"That's what I tell myself," Karen said with a sigh. Her voice wobbled as she gave in to that insecurity she'd mentioned. "You don't think I'm tackling too much, do you?"

"If anyone can do it, you can."

"But can anyone do it? Can anyone be a wife, a mother and a lawyer and do all three jobs well?"

"I don't see why not, as long as you recognize the limitations and deal with them as they pop up. You've done well so far, haven't you?"

"The baby's not born."

"But Dan will be there to help you. He's been supportive from the word go. He wants the baby as much as you do and he knows how much your career means to you. That could make all the difference, Karen—having a husband who's behind you."

"Mmm, I am lucky, I suppose."

"I *know*. So. Do you feel any better?"

"Yeah. It's good to be able to let off steam, but I feel guilty bitching all the time to Dan."

"Your bitching isn't so bad."

"That's cause you're used to it. And because I'm the only little sister you have."

Caroline glanced at the microwave clock. "Don't you think it's time you got some sleep, little sister?"

Karen sighed, but it was a sheepish sound this time. "Yeah, I think I should get a little sleep. Thanks, Caro. You always do make me feel better."

Caroline thought about that for several minutes after she'd hung up the phone. She was glad her sister believed in her, because she was wallowing in her own quagmire of guilt—guilt that she wasn't in Wisconsin helping her mother, guilt that she couldn't spare Carl and Diane their pain, guilt that she could freely build her own career while her sister struggled so hard. She wished she didn't take their troubles so personally, but she always had and feared she always would.

She wondered what her colleagues would say to that. No doubt they'd say she had very strong maternal instincts. They might also suggest that she fostered her family's dependence by being on twenty-four-hour call. If so, she'd been doing it for so long she wasn't sure how to break the cycle.

Rising from the chair, she went to the window. Tall-Dark-and-Handsome was still on his fire escape. She felt a little better.

*Do I do that—encourage their dependence?*

*I don't know. Do you?*

*I suppose. Maybe it is a need I have.*

*Maybe the need is for a family of your own.*

*But in order to have a family of my own, I have to have a husband. If I don't find the right man, I'll be complicating things that much more. I've seen what can happen if a marriage isn't right. The guilt feelings are worse. I'm so tired of the guilt.*

*Come on, where's that optimism?*

Her lips curved at one corner. *Gone with the wind?*

*Sorry. No wind tonight.*

She drew her hand across her cheek, catching rivulets of sweat before they dripped to her jaw. *Tell me about it.*

*No wind. No air. Just us. So what are we going to do about it?*

*I don't know. I don't know.*

*We have to do something. We can't go on meeting this way.*

*But what if we don't get along when we come face-to-face? Things will grow awkward. I won't be able to talk with you the way I have.*

*Ahh, but what if we do get along? Think about it.*

Caroline thought about it all that night and well into the next day. She thought about it while she wound her way up one supermarket aisle and down the next. She thought about it when she was having her hair trimmed, when she was buying stockings, when she splurged on a new sundress that was a little too casual for work. She thought about it while she was at the laundromat and later while she cleaned the loft.

And she thought about it when she was out with Elliot, which compounded her guilt all the more.

# 4

IF ELLIOT WAS PERTURBED when she staved off his advances after dinner Saturday night, he didn't press the issue. She almost wished he had. She was feeling worse and worse about leading him on, but she didn't have it in her to bring things to a head. She knew that she should free him—force him—to see other women, but she dreaded having to do it. Elliot was a kind soul with a fragile ego, particularly when he was on edge at work.

Ben's showing up unannounced on Sunday evening didn't help. She'd been trying to work—between glances at Tall-Dark-and-Handsome's apartment—and the interruption was unwelcome. Tall-Dark-and-Handsome had had his own guest, a petite and attractive woman whom he'd soon ushered back to the door, and Caroline had wanted to study him in the aftermath of the visit. But Ben had come.

"Nice place, Caro," he said, glancing around from the door.

"Thanks. I like it."

"All you need is an air conditioner and it'd be perfect."

"It's fine without," she said, clasping her hands at her waist. She was feeling awkward about not inviting him in, but she didn't want him in. Besides, there was her image to consider. Tall-Dark-and-Handsome might be watching. She didn't want him to think that she had a whole string of men.

With characteristic pertinacity, Ben barged forward. Short of physically restraining him, there was little she could do.

"How about a cool drink?" he asked. The look he sent toward the kitchen said that he wasn't planning on taking her out.

She gestured toward the table, where her files lay open. "I'm really busy, Ben. You should have called ahead and saved yourself the trip."

He shrugged and started wandering around. "I was in the neighborhood. I wanted to see your new place."

Standing beside the open door, she followed his progress. He nodded at the prints she'd hung on the wall, tested the toe of his tasseled loafer against the small area rug before the sofa, ran his well-manicured fingers along the back of the armchair. "Same furniture. It fits in well."

"I thought so."

His gaze idled on the bed. "We had some good times there."

She remained quiet.

"Didn't we?" he asked, facing her.

"Uh-huh."

"At least we agree on that."

"Ben, I really have to work."

His blue eyes grew more so. "You're looking good, Caro. There's something alluring about a T-shirt and shorts. Maybe no air conditioning is a plus."

She could have been the first to say that he looked good in his sport shirt and slacks. He was as cool as ever, despite the three-floor walk up and the warmth of her apartment. Benjamin Howe didn't sweat. Ever. Nor did he affect her the way he once had. The last thing he needed was encouragement, so she said nothing, simply continued to eye him.

"Are you afraid of me?" he asked.

"Of course not."

"You're looking wary."

"I'm just waiting for you to take the hint and leave. I don't know how much more blunt I can be," she said, but innate affability took the edge off her words. "I do have work to do."

"Really?"

"Really."

"And you really want me to leave?"

"Yes."

He sliced another glance to the bed, then skimmed her body from head to toe. His message couldn't have been more clear if he'd written it in blood. "Not even a quickie . . . for old times' sake?"

That was too much. "Don't be crude!"

"Crude, or honest?"

"You'd think that was all we'd had!" Then her lips thinned and she nodded slowly. "But it was, wasn't it? Only there was a lot of other garbage parading as something else that went along with it. Well, I hate to be the one to tell you this, but some women get tired of garbage. I've cleaned house since you left."

"So you don't want the garbage. How about the sex free and clear?"

"No way."

He arched a single brow. "Not even with Mencken, or Malken, or whatever the hell his name is?"

"Not even with him."

"Well," Ben said, grinning, "at least now I know. Okay." He sauntered toward the door. "I'll leave you to your work. If you get lonely, you'll know where I am."

She was bristling with fury, but she refused to let it show. "Goodbye, Ben," she said calmly.

He nodded as he stepped into the hall. With measured movements, she closed the door, then leaned back against it for a minute, took several deep breaths and looked across the courtyard. The sight of Tall-Dark-and-Handsome leaning against his window was an instant balm.

*Ben's nothing but a pest,* she assured him.

*I hope so.*

*And your visitor?*

*No one important.*

A sigh of relief slipped through her lips. *I really do have to get this work done. Did you finish the Sunday paper? If not, you could bring it over here and read while I work.*

*Thanks, but I've got work to do myself.*

*Want to bring it over?*

*I'd like that, but I don't think we should.*

*Why not?*

*Because you'd be a distraction. I'd keep looking at that bed of yours and thinking that we ought to be there.*

*But we don't know each other.*

*Do you honestly believe that?*

Caroline hung her head for a minute and ran a finger over the moisture of her nose. *No. I don't believe it.* She looked up. *But I meant what I said to Ben. I don't want the garbage. I can't handle it right now. Maybe what I do want is pure sex.*

*It'd be more than that with us. And there'd be no garbage.*

*Are you sure?*

*Yes.*

She smiled sadly. *That's a lovely thought, but it's only a dream, and I do have work to do.*

*Okay. Another time, then.*

With a chuckle, she pushed away from the door. *Another time.* That was the nicest thing about a fantasy, she decided, as she sat down and focused on the notes she'd written earlier. A fantasy didn't suffer with postponement. It was always there, a carrot that dangled sweetly and in secret, to be called forth again and again and again.

CAROLINE CALLED FORTH that fantasy many times in the next few days. But even aside from the fantasy, she learned a great deal about Tall-Dark-and-Handsome.

He very definitely lived alone. Aside from his visitor on Sunday—and she dropped in again on Tuesday evening but left as quickly—he seemed a private sort. Except where Caroline was concerned. It occurred to her that he made no attempt to shield his apartment from her view, which made her feel a little less guilty that she did the same.

He ran. Some nights he came home wearing a business suit, changed into a tank top and shorts and went out, only to return after an hour looking tired and sweaty but healthy. Other nights, when he came home, his shirt was wide open and he was already sweaty. She wondered if he'd come from a health club.

He worked. She could see him poring through papers during the evenings—papers of the file type, rather than the newspaper type—and though she continued to speculate on his occupation, the specifics came to matter less than the fact of his diligence.

He didn't drink beyond that one beer an evening; at least, not that she could see. He didn't own a television, or if he did, he rarely watched it. She couldn't tell if he had a stereo; she never once heard the noise. And occasionally she could see him reading a hardcover book.

Sometimes he talked on the telephone, and then she was a little uneasy, for she sensed he was talking with a woman. His expression was gentle, understanding, often beseeching. She doubted it was the same woman she'd seen, since these calls lasted longer than the visits ever had. She told herself that if there was another woman in his life, surely that woman would appear. When she didn't, Caroline could only imagine that she existed, and that was nearly as bad as what she imagined on the nights he didn't return home until late.

It wasn't that she was jealous. She had no claim on the man. It was more that she feared she'd lose him, which was absurd, since she didn't have him to start with. It was all a fantasy, she reminded herself, but that didn't help when she sat at her window staring into his dark apartment. She missed him during those times, just as she welcomed him when he returned. Not a night went by that he didn't come to the window at whatever time he got home.

It became a ritual—a welcome home, a shared drink, a sweet good-night. She had come to depend on it, as they reached what she thought of as their first-week anniversary. When Friday night rolled around, she was particularly needful of that silent shared drink.

She'd had a rough week. The heat had held up—an unusually static high-pressure system, said the weatherman—and she hadn't slept well on many of those nights when the air in her apartment had been hot. It was hot tonight, too. She'd changed into shorts as soon as she'd come home and was reclining against the window, a glass of iced tea in her hand, while Tall-Dark-and-Handsome took his beer from the fridge.

He wore a charcoal tank top over lighter gray running shorts, which, despite their color, made his hips look sleek and narrow. He paused only to take a quick swig of beer and kick off his sneakers before sliding onto the fire escape.

*Hi,* she thought breathlessly.

*Hi, yourself.*

*How was your day?*

He drew away from the wrought-iron railing and flexed his upper back before relaxing again. *Hot. And yours?*

*Ditto.*

*At least it's the weekend. What say we take off and go someplace cool?*

*Like . . . ?*

*Alaska.*

She gave a sultry half smile. *Mmm. That sounds nice. Ever been in an igloo?*

*No, but it sounds real good right about now.* Sweat dotted her neck and pooled between her breasts. She took a drink, then held the cool glass to her cheek.

*Would you really go there with me?* she imagined he'd ask.

*Sure.*

*Don't have any other plans for the weekend?*

*No. I told Elliot I needed a break.*

He put the can to his mouth and tipped his head. In silhouette, his Adam's apple bobbed gently as the cool liquid flowed past. Turning his head slowly, his eyes found hers. *How did he take it?*

*Not well. I feel guilty.*

*You shouldn't, you know. You have every right to refuse an invitation.*

*Still . . .*

*He's a big boy, Caroline.*

*That's the first time you've used my name. I wish I knew what to call you.*

*Tall-Dark-and-Handsome is fine.*

*But it's not real.*

*None of this is real.*

*That's not true.* She sucked in a shaky breath and admitted what she'd been trying to ignore. *What you make me feel is real.*

*Tell me what you feel.*

She pressed her lips together, then slowly moistened them with the tip of her tongue. *Excitement. I look at you and my heart pounds.*

*In this heat?*

*Crazy, I know.*

*What else?*

*Heat inside. I can't really see your face, but your eyes make me sizzle. Or maybe it's the set of your shoulders or the shape of your chest.* She watched him wipe a damp palm on his thigh. *Or your legs. You have beautiful legs. Do you know that?*

*They're not beautiful.*

*Maybe not to you, but to me they are. Lean and tight. They're hairy, too.*

*I'm beginning to sound like an ape.*

*No. Just a hairy man.*

*Do hairy men turn you on?*

*I never thought they did, but the hair on your skin is masculine. So different from a woman's.*

*I should hope so.*

Her insides were beginning to knot. Closing her eyes for an instant, she arched her back, then brought the glass to her forehead. *I don't know why I'm doing this to myself.*

*Maybe you're sex starved.*

*No. Sex is nice, but I've never really hungered for it, if you know what I mean.*

*And you do now?*

*With you. But maybe you don't feel the same way.*

*Are you kidding?*

*You do want me?*

*Why do you think I've got my knees bent up this way?*

*Oh.* The color in her cheeks deepened. *That's nice.*

*It's not nice. It's damn frustrating. What are we going to do about this?*

*I don't know.*

He shifted, straightening one of those knees, seeming to find comfort elusive. Not once did his gaze leave hers; it penetrated the night and the distance between them, searing straight into her heart. *Maybe if we just give in to it and make love, we'll get it out of our systems.*

*Maybe.*

*Should we try it?*

Her breath was coming faster. *I don't know.*

*You could invite me over there.*

She bit her lip. *We're strangers.*

*I could invite myself over there.*

*I don't even know your name.*

*Or you could come over here.*

*I couldn't.*

*We have to break the ice somehow.*

*I know. I know.* She whipped her head toward the door in response to a loud knock. *I don't believe it. Someone's here.*

*Maybe it's Connie.*

She returned her gaze to his. *No. She's gone for the weekend.*

*One of your other neighbors?*

*Maybe.*

*Or Ben. Maybe he's still at it.*

*I hope not.* The knock came again, even louder this time. Again she glanced toward the door.

*You'd better get it.*

*I know.*

*Go on. I'll be here.*

With a sigh of frustration, Caroline set her drink on the window seat and went to the door.

BRENDAN COULDN'T take his eyes from her. She looked so sweet, so agile as she trotted across the floor. And sexy. Her shorts were short, but her thighs and bottom did them proud. And that T-shirt . . . If she was wearing a bra, he'd eat his hat. Not that he owned a hat, but the bet stood; he was that sure of winning. Her hair was caught up in a clasp that left loose strands caressing her damp neck. He could think of all kinds of things he'd do with those loose strands and her neck and his tongue.

Damn. It wasn't a neighbor. It was the guy she dated, but she didn't look pleased to see him. She had a tight grip on the doorknob, and her back had stiffened. Brendan's eyes narrowed. He could see that the man was talking, gesturing toward the inside of her apartment. She shook her head, but he ignored her and took several steps into the loft.

Brendan felt his body grow tense in ways vastly different from the sexual tension of moments before. He watched closely. Her guest continued to talk. She shook her head again, more slowly this time, but whatever she was saying seemed to annoy the fellow, who proceeded to rake a hand through his hair, then fling his arms wide in frustration.

Brendan could almost sympathize with the man. He didn't look like a mean sort; he was clean, nicely dressed, and there was a defensiveness about him. If he was half as hung up on her as Brendan was himself and she was denying him what he most wanted, Brendan could indeed understand the frustration.

His feelings of sympathy vanished, though, when the man clasped her arm. She quickly pulled from his grip and took a step toward the door, but her visitor kept pace, kept talking, kept gesturing. She pointed to the door. The man shook his head. When he snaked an arm around her waist and brought her body flush with his, she arched away and tried to push.

The harsh sound of the beer can crushing in his hand brought Brendan to life. He'd seen enough. Sweet-and-Sexy didn't want that man there. If the guy wasn't willing to accept that on his own, Brendan intended to help him.

Blindly pitching the can toward the sink on his way out the door, Brendan flew down the three flights in record time. He didn't have to pause when he reached the street; he'd traveled the route in his mind so many times that he knew the fastest way around the block. He also knew that since her apartment faced his, her town house had to be the fourth from the corner. He ran there full speed and yanked the door open. When it collided with his toe, he swore, but that was the extent of his self-indulgence. Ignoring the pain, he took the steps two at a time.

He might have taken it as a good omen—to his fantasy or his calculations or whatever—that the door to the third-floor apartment stood open, but he wasn't taking time to think of omens, good or otherwise. He slowed his pace and jogged to the door, coming to a full stop with his hand high on the jamb before calmly ambling inside.

Caroline's head shot to the door the instant he appeared. She'd already freed herself from Elliot's hold, but the threat of his presence remained. Now, abruptly, it was gone and forgotten.

Tall-Dark-and-Handsome? It had to be! The way he looked at her spoke of all she'd imagined and then some.

"Hi, hon," he said softly. Strolling to her side, he wrapped an arm around her shoulder and pressed a warm kiss to her forehead. "Sorry I'm late. I took a detour. Nearly got lost." He gave her a smile and a squeeze, then released her shoulder and extended his hand to her guest. "Brendan Carr. And you are . . . ?"

Elliot stood very still. Only his eyes moved, jumping from Brendan to Caroline and back. He looked totally confused, all but paralyzed, and seemed to be rescued in the end by nothing more than the reflex of manners.

"Elliot Markham," he said, letting his hand be shaken.

"Nice to meet you," Brendan said, then headed for the refrigerator. "Man, is it a warm night." He pulled open the door, extracted the pitcher of iced tea that he knew was always there, took a glass from the adjacent cabinet and poured himself a drink. "Anyone else want some while I'm at it?" he asked, shooting a glance over his shoulder.

Caroline could only manage to shake her head. Her eyes were wide, glued to Brendan—*Brendan*—and she doubted she could swallow air, let alone tea.

Elliot wasn't quite as awestruck. Recovering from the shock of Brendan's appearance—more than that, from the shock of Brendan's obvious familiarity with Caroline's apartment—he narrowed his eyes on Caroline and murmured under his breath, "What's going on here?"

Under normal circumstances, Caroline would have shrugged. But these weren't normal circumstances. Brendan, her hero, had come to her rescue. She couldn't take her eyes from him as he calmly downed his drink and set the empty glass on the counter.

"I asked you a question, Caroline," Elliot said in that same low murmur.

Her eyes flew to his and she blinked, as though surprised to find him still there. "Excuse me?"

"What's he doing here?"

In that instant, Caroline realized that she had to pick up the ball. Brendan's entrance had been stupendous. She couldn't flub her part and let him down. "He's just come in from a run."

"In his bare feet?"

"It's the newest trend," Brendan injected nonchalantly. "I think it started with Zola Budd in the Olympics." He dropped his gaze to the toe that hurt like hell and was beginning to swell. "I have to admit that it has its drawbacks."

Caroline, too, saw the toe. "How did you do that?" she asked, raising hurting eyes to his.

It was all he could do to think of a response when she was looking at him that way. Her eyes were brown, like his. He'd never thought his own particularly scintillating, but hers were. And so soft. And filled with worry.

"I'm afraid—" he made a face and scratched the back of his head "—that I wasn't watching where I was going. There was this Lamborghini that passed me and I made the mistake of turning my head to look at it. I ran into a trash can." He shrugged. "I suppose I could blame it on the dark—"

"Let me get some ice."

"No, no, hon, it's okay." He came to stand by her shoulder, close enough for her arm to graze his chest. "Will Elliot be joining us for dinner?" he asked softly.

Elliot was staring hard at Caroline. "I thought you said there was no one else."

"There hasn't been—"

"—until now," Brendan finished.

"We've just recently met," she explained, but she didn't feel guilt. She knew that would come later. For now, she couldn't think of anything but the large, firm body beside her. Its warmth, a world apart from the June heat, drew her closer. Its scent, ripe with maleness and sweat, filled her senses. Its sheer size made her feel safe and alive and very, very feminine. "Brendan lives across the courtyard," she added a trifle breathlessly.

Mistaking breathlessness for weakness, Elliot lashed out. "You told me that you needed a break this weekend. That you wanted to be alone. That you had work to do and sleep to catch up on. Is this what I get for squiring you around town for three months straight?"

"No one asked you to do that," she said quietly.

"But I did it, and you didn't say boo. Now, all of a sudden you don't need me anymore, so you throw me every excuse in the book."

"I meant what I said."

"Is that why he's here?" Elliot shot back with a dagger's glance at Brendan. "How do you think this makes me feel?"

Caroline knew how Brendan's presence made *her* feel—warm inside, a little giddy and very excited. Because of those feelings she was having trouble sympathizing with Elliot. "I'm sorry if you're upset."

"Upset?" He started to raise a hand to his face but dropped it before it reached its goal. "That's a mild word for what I feel."

Brendan leaned closer to Caroline. His arm crossed her back, hand coming to rest on her arm in light possession. He liked the way her slender body felt by his, liked the smoothness of her skin, the gloss of her hair, the faint floral scent that was so in keeping with his dreams. Most of all, he liked the fact that she was no longer a dream but real.

"Maybe you'd better leave," was his quiet suggestion to Elliot.

But Elliot didn't hear. He was too busy working himself into a self-righteous rage. "I don't deserve this, Caroline. For three months I've been indulgent. I've let you call the shots. If you wanted to see a particular show, I took you. If you wanted to eat at a particular restaurant, I took you. When you were busy with work, I said, 'Okay. I respect you for that.' Where's the respect I deserve in return?"

"Elliot, please don't," Caroline said.

"Why not? Do you find the truth unsettling?"

What he had said wasn't exactly the truth. She knew that he was trying to save face in front of Brendan, but, in his indignation, he was digging the hole deeper. "Nothing will be accomplished by—"

"Shouldn't I fight for what I want?"

"Is that what you were doing just before I got here?" Brendan asked, his low voice cutting through the air like the purr of a whip.

Elliot grew rigid. His eyes widened. He opened his mouth and shut it in the same breath.

Caroline turned her head to meet Brendan's gaze, then promptly forgot both his words and Elliot's presence.

Brendan was beautiful. She couldn't think of another word, and she knew that an impartial observer might think her daft, but she didn't care. His jaw was firm, square and covered by the dark shadow she'd come to expect. But she hadn't expected the tiny white scar on his chin, or the quick softening of his lips when she'd turned, or the faint crookedness of his nose. And though she'd hoped that his eyes would be brown, she hadn't expected that they would be like thick, rich velvet, stroking her deep inside. She hadn't dared hope that they would hold such longing.

He gave a tiny, secret smile. *Hi, Caroline.*

She returned both the smile and the greeting. *Hi, Brendan.*

*Did we finally do it?*

*I think so.*

His hand left her arm. The backs of his fingers lightly brushed her cheek. Her lips parted. She tipped her head until those lips touched his thumb.

"Shit, I don't need this!" Elliot growled.

Jolted by the intrusion, Brendan and Caroline whipped their heads around in time to see him stomp to the door, grab the knob and slam it shut on his way out.

Then, more slowly, they looked back at each other.

"Hi," he said aloud. His voice was nearly as velvety as his eyes, but a smokiness underlay that velvet to produce something extraordinarily manly.

"Hi," she whispered. Standing there, looking up into his eyes, she nearly melted. Her limbs liquefied; her blood flowed faster. Any tension that Elliot's angry departure had caused seemed to gather, break apart, float away.

Brendan's gaze shimmered over each of her features. "I was beginning to think it would never happen."

"Me, too."

"I didn't plan it this way."

"I know."

"But I couldn't just sit there and let him paw you."

She knew that she'd been far from helpless, but that didn't matter. "I'm glad you came," she said, then, unable to resist, raised a hand to his jaw. His beard was rough and spoke of strength. She shaped his lean cheek with her palm and whispered her thumb over his chin.

He closed his eyes for a minute. When he opened them, they were darker. "Your touch is gentle. Nice."

"I kept imagining what you'd look like." Her fingers crept to his lips. Her eyes crept higher, meeting his in a wordless expression of admiration.

The compliment touched him to the core. She made him feel ten feet tall and quivery. He opened his mouth to say something but couldn't think of the words to express what he felt. So, instead of speaking, he touched his tongue to her finger and very lightly put his hands on her waist. Almost instantly, they began a feathery rotation.

Caroline felt the movement clear to her toes. His fingers were long and strong but gently enticing. Dazed with sensation, she closed her eyes and looped her hands over his shoulders. If it was an invitation, it was a subconscious one, but far more than her subconscious felt the glide of his hands on her bare skin as the hem of her T-shirt rose from her shorts. She sighed at the divine pleasure, then sighed again when his lips touched her forehead.

How fantasy paled, she thought. Had she never gone so far as to imagine the way her inner wrists would feel on his shoulders, or the way his chest would press closer with each breath, or the way his thighs would brace hers? She wondered what it was about this man that was so special; then she gave up wondering and simply savored his touch.

Soft. Moist. Sweet. Brendan couldn't believe how perfect she was. He'd held many a woman in his arms in his day, but none had felt so right. Caroline. Her name was as lyrical as she. Caroline. He might have said it aloud, but he didn't know for sure, because the effect she had on him was mind numbing, the pleasure deafening.

He caught a trickle of sweat as it left her hairline and it was on his lips as they moved over her eyes to her cheek. He didn't stop to ask himself if he was rushing things when he sought out her mouth. Hers was waiting and parted.

He kissed her with whisper-soft touches at first, enjoying those exploratory forays. Caroline enjoyed them, too, for her hands had slipped to his back, and the tight cording she found there stood in leashed counterpoint to that gentleness. His tank top was damp, the skin nearby slick with a sweat that lubricated her fingers in their slow journey of discovery. His breath mingling with hers bore the cool, fresh scent of tea. She felt the beat of his heart against her breast, heard its echo in her bloodstream, and she opened herself to him as she had to no man before.

Details blurred then amid an overall air of bliss. Mouths, tongues, hands, bodies—slow, languorous movements gradually speeding with sensual demands. There was heat within heat. The sultriness of the air lent a sultriness to their passion. One kiss led to the next, wider and deeper; one touch led to intimate others. If either of them had been asked if this was a dream, each would have been hard put to answer. The fine line between fantasy and reality ceased to exist.

"I need you," he gasped in a moment's lucidity. Her bare breasts filled his hands; her own hands had slipped beneath the waistband of his shorts and were palming his naked flanks. They were mouth to mouth, chest to chest, belly to belly. His arousal was full, pressed so hard against her that he had to force himself to think. But think he did, even though his voice emerged husky, ragged and rushed. "You know my name, I'm thirty-eight, a lawyer, stable, not married, and I won't give you anything you wouldn't want to write home about except maybe a baby—are you protected, Caroline?"

"Yes," she breathed, "yes."

Within seconds, they'd sunk to the rug. Caroline's T-shirt fell aside, followed quickly by his tank top and then their shorts. They reached for one another, for the only vibrant touch that mattered in that instant out of time.

Caroline had never felt so filled as when Brendan buried himself in her depths. He had never felt so fully received as when she closed herself around him. Though they shared the trust reserved for longtime lovers, each minute, each movement was new and priceless. And whether it was real or imagined, neither could say, but an aura of invincibility gave force to the fire.

The still of the night was broken by soft gasps and breathless sighs, by whispered words of praise and encouragement and, incredibly, by the laughter of two people delighted with themselves and the moment. It was the echo of that laughter that remained long after the gasps had risen to cries and their bodies had erupted in climax.

# 5

THEY LAY ON THE RUG, bodies limp but entwined. Caroline was sprawled half over Brendan, anchored by the dead weight of his arm and one very long, very masculine leg. With her hair tangled, her cheeks flushed and her lips moist and full, she was the image of a woman well loved. He, with half-lidded eyes and a curling grin, was the cat who'd gotten the cream and then some.

"I feel happy," he announced just for the hell of it.

She was every bit as ebullient. "So do I. I should be feeling guilty or embarrassed, even horrified." She raised her head and sought his gaze. "I don't make a habit of going to bed with strange men."

"I am not strange," he assured her as he pressed her head back down. "And we didn't go to bed."

"All the more horrifying. On the *rug*."

He gave a smug chuckle. "Actually, it was nice. Spontaneous. A little unusual, in keeping with our relationship."

"What relationship? We barely know each other."

"We do."

"It's only been eight days."

"Are you kidding? I've been involved with you for weeks."

Her head bobbed up. "Weeks?"

Patiently, he returned her head to his chest a second time. "Weeks."

"But why didn't I know?"

"Maybe because you were too busy. Or because you weren't looking for anything. Or because you're a lady. I'm not."

She grinned against his warm skin. "True. But still, if someone was watching me for that long, I should have felt it."

"Actually, I had reason to start looking," he confessed, and went on to explain about the two girls who had lived in the loft before her. "You are a pleasant turn."

She considered that. "I don't think I've ever been a turn before."

"Forget turn. Think pleasant. Then again, that's a gross understatement."

She grinned again. "If you say so."

"You don't think so?" He was the one to lift his head this time. "Hell, you're spectacular! You handled Elliot perfectly and didn't miss a beat when I arrived."

"I missed a couple right at the start. I never expected to see you sauntering in that way."

"But you knew who I was."

She nodded, then dropped her chin to his chest. "How's the toe?"

"Don't feel a thing."

"That could be good or bad."

"I'll worry about it later."

Her lips twitched mischievously. "How did you really bang it?"

"On the front door downstairs, when I was in such a hurry to rescue you from Elliot." He narrowed one eye. "How did you know I didn't run into a trash can?"

"You wouldn't run into a trash can," she said. "Besides, I knew you hadn't been running. You were in your apartment right up to the point when Elliot arrived, and within five minutes of that you were here." She paused. "You do run, though, don't you?"

"Not as much as I should. Mostly I play racquetball."

"Ahh."

"Ahh what?"

"I was right. Those nights when I'd see you come home looking all grubby with your shirt hanging wide open, I guessed that you were coming from a club."

"If I had any brains, I'd shower there. But I always figure it'll be a waste of time, since I'll be sweaty again by the time I get home." Abruptly he looked stricken, almost comically so. Closing a hand over each of her arms, he tried to raise her. "Lord, I didn't think! I haven't showered tonight. How can you stand me?"

She denied his attempt to hold her away by exerting that little bit more force and said in a soothing voice, "I haven't complained, have I?"

"Maybe you're too polite."

"And maybe I have a head cold." But they both knew it wasn't so, which made her point. "Relax. I like the way you smell."

Given her obvious sincerity, he did relax. Rather, he tried, but the directness of her gaze did something to him. It seemed to enter through his eyes and move downward, squeezing his heart, buzzing his stomach, settling with a hot thud in his loins.

"Ever think of getting an air conditioner?" he asked. It was the first thing he could think of to say, and even then his voice sounded odd.

"Yes, and decided no."

"Me, too."

"How long have you had your loft?" she asked, feeling slightly muddled herself. The husky sound of his voice, the solidity of his long body, the same scent he'd worried about—all conspired to stoke the desire she'd thought sated. And when she looked at him—looked him directly in the eye—she was lost.

"Two years." His hand began to move on her back, palm light, long fingers gliding over silk-smooth skin. "I had another place before that, but it wasn't half as nice."

"Me, too. I can walk to work now."

"What do you do?"

She inhaled a deep breath and rubbed her nose against his chest, then found that so delightful that she repeated the move with her cheek. His skin was warm, lean over muscle, softened by hair. And he smelled...so...good.

"Caroline?"

She raised her head. "Hmm?"

It was a minute before he remembered what he'd been asking. He had to clear his throat before any sound emerged. "Work. What do you do?"

"I'm a family therapist."

He smiled somewhat distractedly and murmured, "A helping profession. I figured something like that."

"You did?"

He nodded, but very slowly. He was enchanted by the way her brows went up, widening her eyes. And those eyes...good Lord, he could drown. "It's the way you walk," he said in a sandy voice.

"It can't be."

He nodded again and as slowly.

"That's crazy," she whispered. She was propped up on a hand that covered that faint rise of his chest, and she'd discovered that the slightest movement not only ruffled his chest hair but brought his nipple to a peak against her palm.

Brendan shifted her gently until she was more fully atop him. His hands formed Vs beneath her arms, supporting her upper torso. His eyes slid from her mouth to her neck, then slowly, helplessly, drifted lower. "Not crazy. You walk lightly and quietly—" he took an unsteady breath "—but there's a gentleness in your stride and a gracefulness in your legs. And—" his eyes grew smoky "—patience. You exude patience, all round and creamy, tipped with rose—"

"My legs?"

"Your breasts." With ease and fluidity, he raised her until one of those breasts met his mouth, which latched on and began a sucking motion that brought a sweet cry to her lips.

"Caroline." His voice was hoarse around her budding flesh. "Caroline what?"

She sucked in her breath and managed a strangled "Cooper," as he tongued her nipple.

It was a minute before he spoke again, and then it was in the thickest of whispers. "I want you again, Caroline Cooper. Slower this time. I want to savor every... single...sweet...spot." He punctuated each word with gentle nips that left her a writhing mass of awakened sensuality.

They did go more slowly this time, and Brendan wasn't the only one to savor the details. While he worshiped her breasts, she ran her fingers through the vibrant tangle of his hair. While she delineated the virile contours of his chest with her mouth, he familiarized himself with the ivory sheen of her shoulders and back. While he explored her legs and thighs with hands that trembled, her own, trembling, too, discovered the flatness of his belly and the smooth, soft skin by his groin.

The time for fantasy had passed. Everything they touched and tasted and felt was real. They flowed around and about each other, seeming suspended in time and space, yet acutely aware of each slow caress. The sweat that covered their bodies was an erotic conduit; the heat in the room was forgotten, overshadowed by the heat of desire.

But there was a price to be paid for slowness. Their limbs began to quake with the burden of harnessed desire. Sweet torture, pleasure and pain, contorted their features. Anguished cries tore from their throats.

When he could stand no more, Brendan turned them so that they were on their sides facing each other. He slid a leg between hers, then a hand to fill the gap he'd opened.

At the first such caress, Caroline tightened her arm around his neck. She needed to hold on; the world seemed to be falling away with sudden speed. She didn't know if it was the newness of Brendan that was so exciting, or if her reaction to him was pure chemistry, or if there were deeper factors at work. She did know that his most gentle touch was frighteningly intense—and that she needed more. With a low whimper, she arched closer.

"Is it good?" he whispered as he watched a myriad of expressions cross her face. By concentrating on those expressions and on the sheer act of speech, he was hoping to stave off his own hunger a bit.

She nodded. Another whimper slipped out.

"You're very soft there." His fingers slid lower. "And moist here."

She whispered his name, nothing more, but the wonder that filled her eyes was all the encouragement he needed.

He continued his low crooning. "Do you know what it does to a man to touch a woman here? Such a private place. And here." His finger entered her with ease and was quickly joined by a second. "No, no, don't shut your eyes."

"I can't help it. . . ." Barely a whisper.

"Look at me, Caroline."

Only with great effort did she manage to obey. She felt dizzy, on a drugless high that threatened to blow her mind. Her fingers bit into his shoulders, and her whisper was broken. "When you do that to me . . ."

He repeated the slow inner stroking. "This?"

She groaned. "It's not enough."

"What do you want?"

She lowered one hand and touched him.

The effect was like fire. He jerked, took several quick, shaky breaths and knew that he couldn't last much longer. Her fingers surrounded him, knowing just what to do. He was almost as moist as she and from the same cause. Still he spoke, albeit in a voice rough with strain. "Do you want me inside?"

She gave vigorous nod. Her lips formed his name, then went on to whisper, "Now!"

"My tongue?"

"Oh!" she cried. The image he evoked was too strong. With a loud indrawn breath, she stiffened, then began to pant with the force of the inner explosion he'd caused.

But the image had worked on him, too, or maybe it was the feel of her hidden flesh pulsing, or the closeness of her body. Within seconds, he'd withdrawn his hand, rolled her over and surged inside. The last of her spasms was more than enough to send him into euphoria. But that was only the beginning, for no sooner had that climax passed than they worked together toward another, then another.

It was a long time before either of them was able to breathe with any degree of steadiness, and a lot longer before either spoke. Between utter exhaustion, intense satisfaction and the enervating heat of the night, they couldn't move. The silence seemed enough.

"Powerful," Brendan whispered at last. His breath couldn't begin to ruffle her hair, which was dripping with sweat but no more so than his own, which clung to his forehead.

Caroline made a sound that was part hum, part moan, entirely in agreement with his assessment.

"In all my dreaming I never imagined it quite like this," he added.

"I never let myself go half as far."

"You dreamed, too?"

She gave another agreeing hum.

"Tell me what you dreamed."

"I dreamed that you were tall and dark and handsome," she said, nestling more comfortably against him. "And you are."

"I could argue, but if you think so, that's enough. What else?"

"I thought your nose would be straight."

"Sorry."

"And that you'd be aristocratic."

"Oops."

"No problem. In my dream, you'd renounced all that decadence, so the end result is the same."

"That makes me feel better. What else?"

"That you were in your late thirties. I was on the button there."

"I dreamed that you were twenty-eight."

She tipped her head against his arm and awarded him a grin. "I like that."

"Was I right?"

"Nope."

"Twenty-seven?"

"What a diplomat you are."

"Okay. How old?"

"Thirty-one."

"You're kidding."

"Nope."

"The body I just ravished has been around that long?"

"Now, wait a minute. I'm not exactly Methuselah. And who are you to talk? You have seven years on me."

"Which is just about right, don't you think?"

She caught in a breath, then let it out in a soft "Yes."

He seemed very pleased with that. "Okay. Go on. What else did you dream?"

"That you were a doctor or a teacher." When he raised a hand, thumb down, she hastened to add, "But a lawyer's okay. My sister's a lawyer. I can take it."

"Thank heavens for that."

"What kind of law?"

"Criminal work."

"À la Perry Mason?"

"Not quite. I work for the Justice Department."

"Do you now?" she asked with enthusiasm. Mentally she shifted the white hat from the head of a doctor or teacher to that of a loyal government employee.

"'Fraid so."

"Why afraid? I think it's great."

"There are many who'd disagree," he said, thinking of one in particular, then quickly pushing her from his mind. "There is a stereotype of government bureaucrats sitting at their desks shuffling papers."

"Is that what you do?"

"I often sit at my desk, but the only shuffling of papers I do is to organize one file and move on to the next."

"What's in the files?"

"Investigation reports, witness statements, a million documents. I work full-time on domestic terrorism."

"Bombings?"

"Those and kidnappings and scores of other crimes or would-be crimes."

She couldn't quite hide a shiver. "Sounds frightening."

"In the sense of the crimes being real, it is. Would that I were out of a job."

In spite of the subject matter, she had to smile. She'd said something very similar to Ben when he'd been so blithely commenting on her work, and it warmed her no end to know that Brendan shared her feelings. That warming livened her curiosity.

"I don't usually think of terrorism in relation to this country."

"Most people don't. Maybe that's because the most brutal acts of terrorism are still committed abroad. I'd like to think that the way this country's run has something to do with that. We're more vulnerable abroad, because we don't have the same controls there that we do here."

"Controls and democracy—a strange pairing."

"Not really. The Declaration of Independence pledges to protect the rights of our citizens to life, liberty and the pursuit of happiness. Certain controls are necessary to protect those rights. The occasional traveler may complain about the security measures in airports, particularly when he's stopped and searched for whatever set off an alarm, but, by far, the majority of us understand that our own safety is at stake. We appreciate the measures taken to secure it."

Caroline had been watching him as he talked and was fascinated. He was articulate, never slipping into the legalese some lawyers hid behind. He was also sincere. Honesty radiated from his eyes, and the relaxation of his mouth reflected his ease with his thoughts.

"Don't look at me that way," he whispered. "It turns me on."

She blinked once, unaware of what she'd been doing. "I'm sorry. I didn't mean to do that. It's just that you have such strong conviction. It's written all over your face."

What was written all over her face was admiration, but it wasn't the kind that an empty-headed woman showed for a man snowing her with rhetoric. It was grounded in respect, and that was what was having such an effect on Brendan. It surprised him, actually. He'd never attributed sexual urges to respect. Of course, he realized they were indirectly related; if he respected the woman he was with, the sex was better. But the fact that the look on Caroline's face excited him had deeper implications, ones he wasn't quite ready—or able—to consider just then.

"I think I need a cool shower," he said.

"Is there danger involved?"

"In a cool shower?"

"In what you do. If you're dealing with terrorists, you have to be putting your own life on the line."

The concern he heard in her voice was adding to his woes. Concern . . . a sexual turn-on? He'd never have believed it before, but the proof was growing quickly. He tried to drag up an image of the most dangerous, the most despicable, the most offensive of terrorists. "I don't deal with them directly, not often."

"Do you try cases?" she asked, raising herself to see him better. The movement shifted her legs between his, brought her tummy warmly against his hip and her breasts against his ribs.

"On occasion." He cleared his throat. "Caroline, I do need a shower. How about we take one?" He felt he could handle showering with her better than he could handle lying naked with her. It would be all too easy to make love to her again, when what he really wanted was to talk, which they wouldn't do if they stayed as they were.

Caroline, who'd been totally immersed in thoughts of his work, wasn't quite sure what to make of his sudden wish for a shower. Though the room was still hot, the sweat had dried somewhat on their bodies. She wondered if he was looking for an excuse to get away. Some men wanted to be left alone after sex. He'd seemed perfectly comfortable to lie with her up until now, but maybe restlessness had caught up to him.

Her expression dropped, torn between apology and disappointment. "Am I asking too many questions? You're probably bombarded with the same ones over and over again. I'm sorry. It must get a little tedious . . . but I'd really like to hear more. I haven't known many lawyers. My sister is in corporate work, which is completely different—"

He stilled her babbling with a single, firm finger against her lips. "No, you're not asking too many questions. I'm glad you're interested, and I'll tell you everything you want to know later, but I'm gettin' pretty hard with you snuggling against me like this. I don't want you to think I have a one-track mind, because I really don't. It's just that my hard part doesn't want to listen to my softer parts. In short," he said, catching a breath, "if we don't get off this rug right now, you'll have raw buns tomorrow."

Caroline's cheeks grew red and she said, "Oh," so sheepishly that he gave her a fierce hug.

"Come on," he growled. "Let's shower. I want to know if your water pressure is as lousy as mine."

It was, but that took little pleasure from the time they spent under the spray. They were completely at ease with each other, talking gently as they soaped, shampooed and rinsed themselves.

Brendan was pleased that Caroline showed neither coyness nor modesty. As he'd dreamed, she was comfortable with herself as a woman, and the idea that she was comfortable enough with him to relax in such an intimate, if nonsexual, activity was gratifying.

Caroline was pleased that Brendan, who was very clearly aroused when they first stepped into the shower, made no attempt to slake his need. It wasn't that she didn't want him again, but somehow, being in such close confines yet foregoing sex made a statement that their attraction went beyond the physical. And that was something she needed to know—particularly after Ben's crude words the weekend before.

"Next order of business," Brendan declared, patting his stomach. "Food."

They were out of the shower, dried as much as the humidity would allow, and dressed again.

"I could make something," she offered hesitantly, "but the choice would have to be between a frozen dinner, a peanut-butter sandwich or scrambled eggs. I haven't much else that's fresh. Tomorrow's market day."

He waved aside her apologetic look. "I feel like Chinese. How about I bring in some take-out?"

"Would you rather go to a restaurant?" she asked, but her reluctance to do that was reflected in Brendan's eyes. Neither of them wanted to eat out. They weren't ready to share themselves with the world, air-conditioned or otherwise.

"We'll eat here." He headed for the door. "I'll just run back to my place for some money."

She reached for her purse. "I have money—"

"No way. Besides, you've got fresh clothes on. I want some and—" he paused to send a rueful glance at his toe, which was less swollen than purple "—a pair of sneakers." At the threshold, he turned and looked back at her. *I could be gallant and go by myself, but I don't want to leave you alone. You might start thinking and have doubts about what we've done, and I don't want that. I need more time with you. We have to talk about where we go from here.* "Come with me?" he asked quietly.

Caroline broke into an open smile. She hadn't really wanted to let Brendan out of her sight so soon, and while she'd never have told him that, she was relieved by the invitation. Holding up a single finger, she ran toward the closet for a pair of sandals.

Moments later, they retraced the route Brendan had taken with such haste earlier that evening. By the time they'd reached his apartment, he'd grown sheepish.

"You'll have to excuse the mess." He made an endearing and hurried—hence, futile—attempt to neaten the mail and newspapers that littered the peninsula jutting out by the door. "I wasn't expecting guests."

"It's okay. I already know you're a slob." Physically removing his hands from the mess, she shooed him away. "Go change. I'm starved." She finished neatening the counter, then stood against it and watched while he tugged on a pair of khaki shorts, shimmied into a clean white polo shirt and laced on a new-looking pair of sneakers. Sitting on the bed, he stuck out his foot and said with pride, "I knew I was saving these for a purpose." Then he stood and advanced on her with one hand low on his hip. "And how do you know I'm a slob?"

"I've seen the way you live, Brendan Carr." She tried to be stern faced, but her eyes danced. "You leave clothes on the chair and magazines all over the coffee table, and you rarely make your bed." She cast a glance at the sink. "I was right. Those *are* dirty dishes piled up."

"You must use binoculars."

She shook her head.

"It's really that bad?"

She nodded.

"I'll have to have the cleaning service more often."

She laughed.

"You're enjoying this, aren't you?" he asked, feigning hurt, but when she nodded again, he grinned. "Let's get that food." Throwing an arm around her shoulder, he guided her toward the door.

"TELL ME MORE about your work," Brendan said, dropping a denuded sparerib into the dish Caroline had set out for that purpose. "How long have you been a therapist?"

"Officially, for seven years. I got my degree at Duke and spent four years working in the Raleigh-Durham area before I came to Washington."

"Why Washington?"

Wiping her greasy hands on a paper napkin, she reached for an egg roll. "I've always been intrigued by the capital. When I got wind of an established group looking for an additional member, I jumped at the chance. It's worked out well. My partners have their little quirks, but they're capable therapists and they gave me more than a fair start. Things have built to the point that my schedule is pretty full."

"Hence the long hours doing reports at home each night?"

"Do *you* have binoculars?"

"Nope. Just a knack for putting two and two together. Hardly a weeknight goes by that you don't spend time at this table."

"There never seem to be enough hours at the office."

"But you do work late there some nights." He was watching her plate as she tried to break into the egg roll with her chopsticks. "Why don't you just pick it up and take a bite?"

"Because this is where the challenge lies."

"To hell with challenges." He reached for his own egg roll, brought it straight to his mouth and devoured one-third of it in a single, neat bite. After he'd swallowed, he gave her a winsome smile. "That wasn't so bad, was it?"

"You have a bigger mouth than I do."

"True," he said, and continued to smile for a minute. She could match him quip for quip. He liked that in a woman.

"What?" she asked, simultaneously amused and be-mused by his lingering smile.

He shook his head and forced himself to tone down the smile. "Nothing. We're getting off the subject of your work. When I think of family therapy, I picture an entire family sitting around a table yelling at each other with the therapist serving as referee."

She chuckled. "Close. There's no table to sit around, but I do referee at times. Actually, my practice is broader than what you've described. I work with families who can't get along, couples who can't get along, kids who have self-image problems or problems coping with a divorce or a death, fathers who feel left out, single mothers. . . ." She paused for a breath. "The list goes on and on."

"Pretty heavy."

"Sometimes."

"Does it get you down?"

"Sometimes. Well, not so much the subject matter, because I'm one of those who believe that every cloud has a silver lining. What really gets to me is when I can't reach a client or when outside factors come into play that ruin the momentum of what I feel has been productive therapy."

"Such as . . . ?"

"When a parent gets tired of paying the bill. He sees a superficial improvement in his child's behavior and decides that, presto, the problem's gone. I'm not one to carry on therapy ad nauseam, but superficial changes are superficial. It's like taking penicillin for a strep infection; the symptoms disappear after the first few days, but if the patient doesn't continue to take the full ten days' worth or whatever, the deep-down germs live on."

"When the problems recur, do you see the child again?"

"Once in a while. Usually I'm the scapegoat. The parent tells himself that I did a poor job and goes to another therapist. I've had clients who've already seen other therapists come to me with the same premise."

"Do you take them on?"

"How can I not?"

"You're a softy."

"My own words exactly," she said with a grunt as she stabbed at the egg roll in frustration. Her delicate picking had done nothing but shred the wrapper. "My heart bleeds easily." She raised the mangled piece of food with her fingers. "Too easily." She bit into it as Brendan had done to his. She wasn't quite as neat; half of the stuffing fell to her plate. "Right about now," she said, then waited until she'd swallowed what was in her mouth before continuing, "I'm feeling badly for Elliot."

Brendan had felt it coming. Strangely, though, he didn't feel threatened. He did feel curious. "What does he mean to you?"

"He's a friend. Nothing more. Tonight was a blessing in some ways. I've been tactfully trying to give him the hint for a while, but he hasn't caught on. At least now he knows. He's probably sitting in his apartment, feeling humiliated and very down on himself. Despite his bravado, he's a little weak in the ego department."

"I pretty much guessed," Brendan said through a dry half smile, "that his accusations were lopsided."

She gave a one-shouldered shrug. "Elliot did his best. He made up his mind about what he thought I wanted to do—"

"And you were too polite to argue."

"Not too polite...."

"Too good-hearted, then."

"It's just so...*painful* to disappoint someone that way. His intentions were always good."

"Will you call him?"

Fiddling with the chopsticks and the scraps of egg roll on her plate, she mulled over that possibility. "I think I have to. I'd like to tell him my feelings. It's overdue—I should have said something sooner—but if I can make him feel a little better about things, it'd help."

"You don't think he'll be even more humiliated if you call?"

That hadn't occurred to her, or maybe it had and she'd ignored it. She had to admit to the possibility that, by calling Elliot, she'd be easing her own feelings of guilt far more than his sense of rejection. "Do you think so?" she asked cautiously. "You're a man. What would you want, if you were in Elliot's shoes?"

"That's hard to say."

"Would you feel that I was rubbing salt in the wound?"

He forked in a mouthful of Moo Shu Beef and chewed pensively. "Probably. At least, at the time I would. Later I might realize that what you said made sense. 'Course, that would depend on what you did say."

"That there isn't any future in our relationship, that it could linger for months but that that wouldn't be fair to either of us."

Brendan nodded. "I could probably buy that if I were Elliot, but there's more that he'll want to hear." The inflection of his voice suggested that she'd know what that was, which she did.

"He'll want an explanation for you and me," she supplied with a smattering of guilt.

"Right."

She took a deep breath. "Then I'll just have to repeat what we told him tonight."

"A lot's happened since then."

She dropped her gaze. "I know."

"Are you sorry?"

Her eyes flew back to his. "No!" After a moment's pause, she asked softly, "Are you?"

He shook his head firmly and with finality.

That satisfied Caroline. Out of sheer curiosity, she asked, "Who is the pretty blond-haired woman I've seen at your place?"

Brendan answered in a similarly straightforward tone. It was as though they'd already agreed that the blonde was no threat, simply an incidental to be explained. "Jocelyn. We've dated some. It sounds as though my situation with her is very much the same as yours has been with Elliot."

"She wants more, but you don't?"

"That's it."

"She doesn't take hints."

"Nope."

"And you can't just tell her to get lost."

"Right. She's new around here. A mutual friend back in Detroit told me she was coming and asked if I'd show her around. She's a very nice, very gentle lady. I've been trying to think of men to introduce her to, but the ones I know are either too young, too old, too married or too tough."

"How about you give her Elliot's name?" Caroline suggested tongue-in-cheek.

He answered in the same mischievous vein. "How about you give him her name?"

"On second thought—"

"—we ought to wait a bit. It'd be pretty awkward breaking up and arranging a fix-up in the same breath."

Caroline grinned broadly, then took a loud breath and sat back. "Well, now that we have that problem solved . . ."

"What about the other fellow who was here?" Brendan asked. "The one who stopped by last Sunday."

Her grin faded into something less gentle and she set down the chopsticks. "That's Ben. We were together for a year, but it's over and done. He's been in Spain for six months. I guess he was hoping I'd fill the gap until he could find someone else."

"But you won't."

"Absolutely not."

"Good." He, too, sat back. They continued to regard each other in silence for a minute. Then he said, "Which brings us down to the nitty-gritty. Are we . . . a couple?"

She didn't have to give it much thought. Though their lovemaking played a role in her decision, it was far from the deciding factor. She felt comfortable with Brendan, but more than that, he excited her. There was so much in his eyes as they held hers now, so much in his expression, so much in his mind. She'd be a fool not to explore all those things. And Caroline Cooper was no fool.

# 6

"I'D LIKE THAT . . ." Caroline began.

Brendan worried when her voice trailed off. "But . . . ?"

"I'd like it more than anything. But there's something you ought to know. There have been times lately. . ." She frowned, struggling to verbalize her thoughts. "There have been times lately when I've felt . . . used."

He nearly sighed in relief. For a split second, thoughts of a dire illness or a dark cloud from the past or even an impending move that would take her from Washington had flitted through his mind. "Used" he could deal with, once he knew what she meant.

"By men?" he asked.

"No, no. By . . . oh, Lord, by *everyone*." Her eyes widened emphatically. "Maybe 'used' is the wrong word. It sounds malicious, when there's never been malice intended." She continued to struggle, finally eyeing him helplessly. "But I can't find a better word."

"Just take it slow and tell me what you feel. There's no rush. We have all night."

His soothing tone was a help, and his eyes held all the patience in the world. Encouraged, she began to explain. "When you asked me how long I'd been a therapist, I answered in terms of 'officially.' Do you remember?" He nodded. "Well, unofficially I've been one for nearly twenty years."

"An eleven-year-old therapist?"

She acknowledged the absurdity of the claim with a feeble smile. "Actually, I was probably twelve or thirteen, but it all begins to blur from there. I had a good-sized group of friends, and we were all pretty close. Somehow I emerged as the confidante. They poured their hearts out to me, and I listened and soothed as best I could. My brother and sister—he's a year older, she's two years younger—did the same, and I don't remember when that began. I was the one in the middle, the one with a level head on her shoulders, the Rock of Gibraltar, the Wailing Wall, the Solomon. My brother is a bright guy but he's always been impulsive. He leaps before he looks, then falls apart when something goes wrong. My sister is every bit as bright, but she's always had a talent for biting off more than she could chew. Given that she's a perfectionist and that she can't always meet her own high standards, she ends up tense. It's always been my job to help her work through that tension."

"I would have thought that to be your parents' job," Brendan observed gently.

Caroline shot a helpless glance at the ceiling. "My parents are a whole other story. My dad is the sweetest guy in the world. He runs a successful business and he's a crackerjack at what he does, but when it comes to dealing with other people's emotions, he's helpless. Unfortunately, my mother is a whirling dervish of emotions. She worries about anything and everything. If there aren't any problems, she creates them."

"So your brother and sister turned to you."

"And my mother. She turned to me, too! She'd be right there when I got home from school to tell me of her latest trauma. And I listened and commiserated and said whatever I could to make her feel better." She held up a hand. "Please don't misunderstand me. It wasn't that I had any answers, that I was a genius or anything—simply that I had a positive attitude and some common sense."

"And patience," he said with a smug grin.

She blushed, recalling the observation he'd made while they were making love. "And patience," she admitted softly. She reached for the pitcher of iced tea, refilled both their glasses, then took a long, cool drink from her own.

Brendan was thinking about what she'd said. "You were obviously a born counselor. Your family must have seen that early on."

"I'm not sure that they were aware of what was happening back then. Now they say things like 'I knew I could count on you, Caro,' or 'What would I do without you, Caro?' or 'You're a good soul, Caro.'"

"Now? You mean it's still going on?"

She nodded and scrunched her face up in despair. "My mother still calls me several times a week from Milwaukee, my sister from Philadelphia, my brother from Baltimore. I do love them and I'd be lonely if I didn't talk with them, but to come home from work and have to deal with every one of their problems and nonproblems and worries and fears . . . it's too much. Maybe if I were in a different profession, if I weren't dealing with other people and their problems day in, day out, I'd have emotional energy to spare. But I've begun to feel so *tired* of it all, so—"

"Used."

Her gaze grew beseeching. "Then you understand?" He barely had time to nod when she sat forward and rushed on. "And it isn't only my family. It's my friends. Old ones drop by when they're in Washington, and I love seeing them and exchanging news, but somehow or other we always revert to the same pattern. They pour out their hearts, I listen and counsel. I mean, it's always been this way, so I don't know why it's bothering me now—except that maybe it's finally hit me that there ought to be two sides to a relationship.

"Okay—" she held up a hand "—you're probably thinking that I'm a stable person who solves her own problems rather than seeking out the advice of others, and to a certain extent you're right, but not completely. I have needs, too."

"Do your friends know that?"

"On one level they do, but I don't harp on it. And I know that's my problem, too. If I were to say something or be more demanding, things might be different. But I get so wrapped up in their lives that I don't think of my own until afterward. Take Jessica Wright. We met at an aerobics class two years ago and became friends. I really like her. She works at a local TV station, so she's interesting and she's fun. But her social life is like a soap opera. She called me last month—I still can't believe this— she called me in a panic because she'd mistakenly made dates with two guys on the same day. Now, theoretically she'd have been okay. She was seeing Donald in the afternoon and Malcolm in the evening. Except she'd promised Malcolm dinner at seven, which was just about the time Donald said he'd have her back."

Brendan could anticipate the problem. "But she couldn't say anything to either, because neither was supposed to know about the other?"

She nodded. "Would you believe that both men work at the station?"

He winced, but his thoughts were already moving ahead. "What did she have you do?" he asked cautiously.

"I went over to her place at five, set the table and put dinner on to cook—none of which she could do earlier, or Donald would have suspected something when he picked her up."

"Couldn't she have said a girlfriend was coming over?"

"With fine china, starched linens and candlelight?"

Brendan conceded the point with an appreciative "Not bad. So, what happened then?"

"By the time seven rolled around, I had everything ready. Jessie had Donald drop her at another friend's apartment. She raced through the back alleys and climbed up the fire escape to her bedroom, while I did my best to occupy Malcolm." She combed her fingers through her bangs, which were damp again from the heat. "Forget the fact that I was late for a date myself. Jessie was so apologetic and so grateful that it didn't seem to matter at the time: I told myself that it was one instance, that's all. But if it isn't Jessie, it's someone else." She paused for the quickest of breaths before barreling on. "Take my partners at work. They're all wonderful, and I never mind covering for them when something comes up, but there has to be a limit somewhere, somehow, on their other demands. Maren insists that I take her shopping—"

"You have great taste in clothes."

Caroline didn't have to ask how he knew what she wore, so she asked more softly, "Do you think so?"

He nodded.

The pleasure his compliment brought broke the momentum of her diatribe. She smiled and sat quietly for a minute.

"Go on," he prompted.

Her shoulder settled with the release of tension. "I can't believe I'm doing this. I sound just like my mother."

"You're human. You need to sound off once in a while. When was the last time you did it?"

She shrugged.

"Then it's long overdue. Please. Go on."

She gave a quick shake of her head. "You don't need this."

"Go on."

"I must be boring you silly."

"You're making me feel useful. Besides, there's a message that's coming for me at the end—that 'but' about our future together. Since I'm not sure I want to hear it, the longer you take getting there, the better." He cleared his throat. "Now, then, you were talking about your partner, Maren, with whom you go shopping. I take it she has lousy taste in clothes?"

Caroline sent him a you-should-only-know look. "On top of that, she has bright-red, almost orange hair and she's on the chubby side, so the challenge of finding things that become her is that much greater."

"How about your other partners?"

She raised a finger. "There's Peter, who is a single father and needs a recreation director when his thirteen-year-old daughter is with him, which is every other weekend." A second finger joined the first. "There's Norman, who's at war with his mother-in-law and needs a full-time strategist—and who, by the way, happens to be Elliot's brother, a lovely situation." A third finger went up. "And there's Jason, our part-time secretary, who has discovered that he gets better grades on his college papers after I've done some editing."

"And you can't say no?"

"How *can* I? They're my friends. They need help, so they come to me. They know I won't refuse. But it's been so tiring lately. Always another demand. Maybe it's the heat—" The phone rang. Her gaze flew to the offensive instrument, and her voice dropped to a conspiratorial whisper. "I knew it was too good to be true. Not a call all evening. This one is bound to be a doozy."

Brendan had to work hard to keep from laughing at her beleaguered expression. The phone rang again. "Should I get it?"

She seriously considered that, then shook her head. "If it's Elliot, he'd be crushed." She glanced at the digital clock on the face of the microwave oven. "It's pretty late. With the time difference, though, it could easily be my mother in some kind of dither. Even without the time difference, it could be Karen going into labor, or Carl about to strangle Diane—" A third ring came and Caroline pressed a fist to her forehead. "I can't stand this." Jumping up from the table, she snatched at the receiver. "Hello?"

"Gladys?" asked a slow, elderly male voice.

"Gladys," Caroline echoed in a chagrined whisper, then said full voice, "No, this isn't Gladys."

"Well, may I speak with her?" the man asked haltingly.

She closed her eyes and shook her head, unable to restrain a smile at the humor in the situation. "I'm sorry, but there's no Gladys here."

"Could you . . . tell me when she'll be back?"

She pressed two fingers to her forehead, rotated them in a slow circle. "You misunderstand. No one by the name of Gladys lives at this number."

"What number is this?"

"What number are you calling?"

There was the rustle of paper over the line. Lifting her hair off her neck with one hand, Caroline waited patiently. She looked first at Brendan then at the ceiling.

"Here it is," the man said slowly, and read off the number he wanted.

"You've dialed wrong, sir. Why don't you hang up and try again?"

"Oh, *I'm* sorry," he said in genuine dismay. "My fingers aren't as steady as they used to be. I'm so sorry."

"It's perfectly all right," she said, and hung up the phone. "That's the second time he's called," she told Brendan. "Poor old fellow—he sounds to be close to eighty. Why do you think he's calling Gladys so late at night?"

"Beats me," Brendan said with a grin.

The grin was a little too smug. "Do you *know* that man?"

"Of course not."

"But you know something."

He shrugged. "Just that certain urges are timeless."

Caroline looked doubtful as she returned to the table. "You don't really think that that old man . . ."

Brendan shrugged again. "You could always ask him next time he calls."

"Mmm. Now why didn't I think of that?"

"Because," he drawled, "you're a la-dy."

The smile she tried to hide came out crooked. She didn't know how any man could be as adorable as Brendan. He was sprawled in his chair with his legs crossed at the ankles. He'd long since kicked off his sneakers. His arms were folded over his chest, and his shirt had come free of his shorts. The way he was looking at her made her heart melt, and when he used that playful drawl . . . On impulse, she coiled an arm around his neck, leaned down and planted a wet, loudly sputtering kiss on his beard-shadowed cheek.

"What was *that*?" he asked, pulling her onto his lap.

"A zerbert."

"What's a zerbert?"

"Haven't you ever watched *The Cosby Show*? No, you haven't, because you don't have a television, but I do. When I heard all the hullaballoo about this terrific show, I had to watch it one time. Actually, it was funny enough to tune in more than once, but either I'm not home at the right time, or I'm on the phone, or I don't think to turn on the TV until it's too late."

"So what's a zerbert?"

"It's the thing that Rudy gives Cliff, the thing I just gave you." Levering herself from his lap, she reached for the container of Moo Shu Beef.

"What are you doing?"

"Reheating it."

"You don't like sitting on my lap?"

She was facing the kitchen, with her back to him. At his question, she dropped her chin to her chest. Didn't she like sitting on his lap? A foolish question. Her arms were alive where they'd made contact with his shoulders, and the backs of her thighs weren't the only things still tingling. "I think," she said, letting her head fall back with an intake of breath, "that I could happily sit on your lap for the rest of tonight and most of tomorrow."

"I wouldn't mind that," Brendan murmured in her ear. With barely a sound, he'd come up behind her. The length of his body conformed to hers. His arms framed her sides.

Sighing, she closed her eyes and relaxed her head against his shoulder. "Make that a week," she breathed.

He touched his lips to her temple. "Uh, could be a problem there. I'm supposed to fly to Detroit on Monday."

"For how long?"

"Four days."

"Do you do things like that often?"

"Several times a month."

She turned her head so that her face was against his neck. "Then I won't have your light to look forward to at night?"

"I could buy a timer."

"Not the same."

"You could come with me." He made a low crisscross of his arms on her middle, bringing her that much more snugly against his thighs. "We could do all kinds of naughty things before and after my meetings."

"But I have to work." Of her own accord, she turned and wrapped her arms around his neck. "You're an awesome temptation, though," she said, and met his lowering mouth. His kiss was deep and thorough. By the time he let her up for air, she was clinging to his shoulders for support. "And an awesome kisser," she added breathlessly.

"Look who's talking. Here I am, doing my best to show you that I have drives beyond the sexual, and you move this way or twist that way or come up with an expression that reduces me to a mass of live-wire hormones, when we still have to talk."

The moment's silence was profound. Caroline could clearly feel both his arousal and the tiny tremors caused by the flow of desire through his limbs. She was similarly aroused, though less visibly so, and one part of her wanted nothing more than to reach down and touch him. The other part recognized the truth in his words, and her facial expression acknowledged it.

He took her face in his hands and bent his head until their eyes met. "Tell me you'll sleep with me tonight. I can take all the talking in the world as long as I know that."

"I'll sleep with you tonight."

He sighed in relief, then abruptly shifted gears. Grabbing the carton of fried rice from the table, he set it in the microwave beside the Moo Shu Beef. "How long?"

"Uh . . . uh . . . two minutes?"

He programed in the time, turned on the microwave, then put some very necessary distance between himself and Caroline by walking around the far side of the table and resuming his seat. "Where were we?"

"Kissing."

He punished her with a scowl. "Before that."

"Zerberts?" The teasing was a help. Her heartbeat, racing moments earlier when she'd been in his arms, was gradually returning to normal.

He made a rewinding gesture with his hand.

Caroline complied. "Way back then I was complaining about the people at work. But I need a break from ranting and raving. Tell me about you."

Brendan didn't respond at first. He was trying to gather his wits. From time to time—like now—he caught an overall glimpse of what was happening to him and he was shaken. He couldn't quite believe that Caroline was Caroline and that she was real and that he was suspiciously close to being head over heels in love. The last thought was the most incredible, but he didn't know how else to explain the way his heart seemed to open up and reach for her each time she looked his way.

"Brendan . . . ?"

He blinked once and regained his presence of mind. "You haven't finished telling me about you."

"I'll finish later."

"But I need to hear the moral of your story."

"It'll come."

"You'd leave me in suspense?"

She nodded. "Have you ever been married?"

He wanted to argue more, because, despite the light-hearted tone he worked so admirably to produce, he really *was* anxious to hear what she had to say. But he understood her curiosity. She had a right to it. Hadn't she just agreed to spend the night with him? Besides, it wouldn't hurt to lay his cards on the table at the start.

"No. I've never married. I came pretty close once, but the relationship died a very vocal and angry death."

Caroline tossed a glance toward the window and spoke softly. "When I was . . . fantasizing, I made a list of the reasons why you might still be single."

"How did you know I was—I mean, before tonight?"

"I don't get involved with married men," she said, as though the simple statement answered his question.

"You were planning on involvement?"

"Not planning. Fantasizing. I thought that maybe you'd had an early, unhappy marriage and were divorced. Or that you'd been too involved with your career to marry. Or that you'd never found the right woman." She paused, and her voice gentled all the more. "What happened?"

Before he had a chance to explain, the microwave dinged. She held up a finger, pivoted to remove the containers and set them on the table. Only after she'd doled out first rice, then beef did she give a go-ahead wave with her chopsticks.

Brendan gaped at the mound of food on his plate. "You didn't divvy this up too evenly."

"I just want a little."

"Do you want me to talk or eat?"

"Both."

"That'll be cute."

"You'll find a way."

Indeed, he found that by alternating between talking and eating and looking at Caroline, there was less pain in the telling of his story. "Gwen and I met as first-year law students in Boston. She was different from me—very aggressive, very sophisticated—and I found that exciting. As a couple, we worked well. We saw different sides of issues and argued them through until we'd both benefited from the debate. I had imagination, she had technique. We learned from each other." He took time to eat some, then resumed. "I really thought that was it. We were in love. We'd graduate, get jobs, live happily ever after."

In her customary role now, Caroline listened intently. Brendan had no idea that her heart was beating faster as she waited for the punch line.

"The trouble probably started in the summer before our third year, when we took jobs that theoretically were apprenticeships for what we'd be doing once we passed the bar. Gwen was interning with a corporate-law firm, I was in the district attorney's office. We'd have good-natured arguments—at least, I thought they were good-natured, though some of them were pretty heated—about private practice versus public service. Gwen felt that the true prestige and the only stability were in private practice. I felt that the real respect and the major challenge were in public service. We each had our own, very different convictions, and they became a constant issue between us. Our arguments went on through that entire third year, and toward the end, heated was a mild word to describe them." His features wore the memory without grace.

"So you went your own ways after graduation?"

"Oh, yes. I could have accepted Gwen's work—even though she talked like a fat cat—if she could have accepted mine. But she wanted money, and I knew damn well that as a public servant I'd never earn it in the big way she wanted."

"You were angry."

"Yeah, I was angry. And hurt. I felt as though she'd rejected me for the pettiest of reasons. Then I realized that the reasons weren't petty at all, and the rejection wasn't one-sided. Gwen and I had totally different value systems. The money issue was just the final straw. In hindsight, I'm amazed that we lasted together as long as we did. I could only guess that it was because we were students and living in that kind of limbo."

He paused to eat, but his heart wasn't in it. After pushing a piece of beef around his plate, he set down his fork and raised his eyes to hers. "I live well, Caroline—not extravagantly but well. Over the years I've saved and invested, but I've never been impressed with conspicuous consumption. The loft may be modest by some people's standards, but it suits my needs. I choose to live there. Someday I may choose to live elsewhere. If so, great. Likewise, when I take a vacation, I do it the way I want. That may mean staying in a posh Caribbean resort or in a crude ski lodge, but I have the option of choosing and I exercise it."

Caroline could find no fault with his philosophy, which was similar to her own. Nor could she fault the candor in his eyes, the urgency, the vulnerability. Knowing that he wasn't finished speaking, she remained quiet.

"I guess what I'm trying to say," he went on, propping his forearms on the table, "is that I don't have all the money in the world, nor do I want it or need it. I love my job. Working for the government gives me rewards far beyond green stuff. Sooner or later, this attorney general will resign or be replaced in the natural transition of power, in which case I'll be looking for a new job. Given my record, it won't be a problem. Don't ask me where I'll look, because I don't know. But I do know that I want to remain in public service."

Caroline felt admiration and a great deal of pride. "You sound defensive about it. There's no need."

His eyes were scanners, picking up every nuance of her reaction. "I just wanted you to know."

"Okay. Now I know."

Very slowly, his mouth softened from a firm line to a tentative half smile. "Aren't you glad you asked about marriage?"

She nodded. "It taught me more about you." Her eyes twinkled. "And just for the record, the last vacation I took was a long weekend this past February. I stayed at a farm in Vermont, where I shared a bathroom with eight other guests. We ate family style, sitting around a long table with the couple who owned the farm and their three kids, and we helped pay our keep by doing chores. Mine was to collect fresh eggs from the henhouse."

"Did you enjoy that?"

"I enjoyed walks in the nearby woods better than collecting eggs, but I'd go back to the farm in a minute. It was relaxing. Restful. A nice change of pace."

With a suddenness that startled her, Brendan bolted from his chair, rounded the table, scooped her up and carried her to the window seat.

"What are you doing?" she cried.

"Abducting you. You're perfect. You have the right answer for everything." He lowered himself to one knee on the seat and settled her sideways between his thighs. His arms closed around her, gently locking her in.

"You're abducting me to my own window seat? What kind of an abduction is *that*?"

"You had something else in mind?"

She said nothing, simply slipped her arms around his waist.

He spoke against the top of her head. "Let's go to Maine."

"Hmm?"

"I said let's go to Maine. We can fly up to Bangor first thing in the morning, rent a car and drive north. There are secluded little cabins for rent along the banks of the Penobscot. It'd be quiet and cool."

"That's incredible," she murmured.

"Not necessarily incredible but certainly—"

"No, no." She raised her head until their eyes met. "I don't mean Maine, but the fact that you suggested it. When I was fantasizing, I pictured us doing something like that. I pictured your sweeping me off somewhere where I'd . . . be . . . free of responsibility and guilt." She sucked in a sudden breath. "Brendan?"

He loved the way she said his name. "Mmm?"

"That's the moral of my story. When you ask me if we're together, and I say 'yes, but,' that's what I mean." She responded to the confusion in his eyes by hurrying on. Her own gaze had taken on the same candor, the same urgency and vulnerability she'd seen in his moments before. "If there's one thing I want—no, *need*—in a relationship it's freedom. I'm tired of feeling responsible for people. I'm tired of feeling guilty when I want to do my own thing. I'm so *tired* of the strings and the obligations and the little catches. There are so many hassles in my life. I don't want us to be a hassle." She paused, and the pleading quality in her voice grew even more so. "Can we do it?"

He was quiet for a minute, pensive as he studied her face. At last he said, "I don't know. I'm not sure any relationship can be as free as that. By definition, a relationship implies some kind of tie."

"Mutual attraction is a tie, and that's okay."

"What kind of attraction are we talking—physical or emotional?"

Caroline was in the process of deciding that when his features distracted her. They were honest, open features, inviting honesty and openness in turn. "That's exactly what I want," she whispered. "Honesty and openness. I want to say only what I want and what I feel. I want you to say only what you want and what you feel. No lies. No little fibs or empty platitudes. No game playing. No bartering with vows and promises."

"I can buy that—"

"But there's more. I want to be able to lean on you. I want to be able to complain, to let off steam, to ask for sympathy and advice and coddling. I'm tired of being the mother in relationships. I'm tired of being the caretaker. I want to be the one taken care of—" Her voice broke off sharply.

"What's wrong?"

"I don't believe I'm saying all this," she muttered, averting her eyes. She tried to put some space between them, but Brendan's arms tightened around her.

He could see her embarrassment and touched those telltale spots—her cheeks, her lips, her forehead—with his fingertips. "You're saying what you want. You're being honest and open."

"I'm being selfish."

"Maybe you need to be selfish."

"But I can't expect you to put up with that."

"Why don't you let me decide what I'll put up with and what I won't? Right now, I'm trying to understand exactly what it is you're saying."

Her earnest eyes went to his. "I'm saying that I can't promise you anything."

"You want a straightforward, uncomplicated, pleasure-as-long-as-it-lasts relationship."

Very slowly, she nodded. "I think that's all I'm capable of right now."

"Because you're being pulled in so many different directions?"

"And because I feel used up...burned out...drained."

Brendan didn't have to consider his options. Nor did he have to argue with Caroline about her capabilities. She might tell him that she felt used up, burned out and drained, yet she'd given him more in the past few hours than any woman had given him in years.

"I accept your terms," he declared.

"You do?"

He nodded. "I don't need a mother. Or a therapist. I can't promise to be a yes-man, because that's not me. I can't lie about my feelings and I don't think you'd want that, anyway. But I won't take advantage of you. I won't expect or demand. I'll be yours to use as you want."

Caroline wasn't quite sure what to make of his easy compliance. She'd expected some sort of argument. Or was it that she'd hoped for one?

"You . . . really don't mind?" she asked hesitantly.

"Nope."

Her skepticism lingered for just a minute longer. In the end, it was destroyed by the very selfishness she'd worried about. She had what she wanted. Brendan Carr—secret friend and neighbor, white knight, lover extraordinaire—had agreed to honor the terms of her fantasy.

He was what she needed right now. If he had no complaints, who was she to argue?

"Okay," she said, smiling. "We're a couple."

"How about Maine?"

"I still can't believe you've suggested that. When I was fantasizing, I thought of someplace up north where the nights would be cool. Only I imagined we'd drive the whole way."

He gave a quick shake of the head. "Not enough time. It's a ten-plus-hour drive. We'd have to turn around as soon as we got there and drive right back in order to get to work on Monday. If we fly, we'll have nearly twenty-four hours up there. Do you have anything here tomorrow or Sunday that can't be missed?"

"No."

"Me, neither. So what do you think?"

"I think that I've never thought of doing anything half as impulsive as this before."

"Wrong."

"Wrong?"

He took her face gently in his hands, fingertips tangling with the damp tendrils by her cheeks. "Making love with me earlier tonight was more impulsive, don't you think?"

She blushed and nodded.

"Which goes to show that our impulses are good where each other is concerned, so let's go to Maine."

"Okay."

# 7

IT WAS A LOVELY IDEA, "was" being the operative word. But to have caught a flight to Bangor and allowed for driving time from there would have meant leaving at seven, and at seven that morning Brendan and Caroline were dead to the world. After a night of much loving and little sleep, it was no wonder.

Brendan was the first to awaken. Sprawled facedown on the bed, he turned his head on the pillow, dragged in a sleep-roughened breath, then stretched. His body felt utterly spent, but it was a relaxed kind of exhaustion, a lovely lethargy that spread from his neck to the tips of his toes.

Satisfied. He felt incredibly satisfied. It was a new sensation and it puzzled him, until he managed to pry open one eye and see where he was. Unable to resist when his gaze lowered over a disheveled head of hair, an ivory-smooth back and a softly rounded bottom, he broke into a very slow, very smug, very male grin.

A minute later, the grin vanished and his head popped up. "Oh, no," he whispered, focusing on the nightstand clock. *"Eleven?"*

A soft moan came from Caroline, whose head was tucked by his ribs. She curled a leg sideways and straightened one arm on the rumpled sheet, then, with another moan, reversed each of those movements and slowly turned toward him. He knew the instant that awareness hit her, because she went abruptly still. She extended the fingers of one hand and tentatively touched their tips to his waist. Then, as tentatively and almost disbelievingly, she raised her head and met his gaze.

"We overslept," he said. His voice, still sandy with sleep, held the same element of unsureness that he saw in her gaze. He didn't know whether she was pleased, displeased or indifferent, and the matter of the trip to Maine was the least of it. Hard as it was to believe, when he felt as though he'd known her forever, this was the first time they'd faced each other in broad daylight.

Caroline's only problem was an initial disorientation. She wasn't accustomed to waking up with a man, and his sheer physical presence with its distinct warmth and scent confused her—until she realized that this was Brendan. Her confusion vanished quickly. Brendan. It seemed perfectly natural that he should be in her bed. With the softest of smiles, she lay her forehead on his middle.

"Caroline?"

She yawned.

"Are you okay?"

She hummed a yes.

"I think it's too late to try for Maine."

"S'okay," she murmured. "This is nicer."

He gently twisted her hair off her neck. "Anyway, it's raining."

She hummed another yes.

He wondered if she knew what was going on, because it sounded to him like she was falling back to sleep. At least she seemed content, he mused with another smile as he looked down her prone form.

She was a sprawler like he was. There'd been some tight moments on her double bed during the night, times when, in their sexual abandon, they'd nearly toppled to the floor. Even now he was perilously close to the edge, while she angled out from his side. But he didn't mind.

Lord, was she sweet. Sweet and natural and uninhibited. She was perfectly at ease with him. They were made to be together.

Unfortunately he couldn't tell her that, though every instinct inside him wanted to. She'd think that he was trying to put ties on her, and he'd promised her that he wouldn't. He'd also promised that they'd go to Maine, but he'd broken that one.

"I should have set an alarm," he said in a soft apology to himself as much as to her, then mumbled something resembling "Guess I had other things on my mind."

For someone who was allegedly falling back to sleep, Caroline's good-humored if groggy-sounding "I'll say" was prompt. She knew precisely what Brendan had had on his mind, and she'd been guilty of the same. She couldn't begin to review each single instance when they'd turned to each other during the night. At times he'd been the initiator, at times she had been. Who had moved first hadn't mattered, though, because they'd shared a fierce and endless hunger. Even now, when she opened her eyes to the lean, manly lines of his torso and legs, she felt a stirring inside. Slightly dismayed by that, she stirred the rest of her body, maneuvering up to meet his head on the pillow. She couldn't restrain a moan in the process.

Rolling to his side so that he faced her, he put a hand on her hip. "What's wrong?"

Her cheeks grew pink. "Nothing. Just a little sore."

His hand slid down her thigh, then up its inside. "Here?"

She nodded.

"You haven't been with a man since Ben?"

"No. And I never did this with him."

Brendan's lips twitched. "Marathoning?"

She laughed. It was a soft sound, feather light and gay. "Mmm. I guess that says it." She was quiet for a minute. "Where do you get your strength? You're probably not the least bit sore."

His dark eyes twinkled as they held hers. "I wouldn't say that. I thought I was in good shape, playing raquet-ball and all, but this morning my upper arms and shoulders are protesting something or other I did to them."

She pictured precisely that something or other he'd done, and her skin warmed. "I'm glad to know it's not only me," she said more softly. Looking into those vel-vety brown eyes, she was mesmerized. But it wasn't only his eyes. It was his tousled hair and his stubbly jaw and the breadth of his chest and the fullness of his sex—all of which were powerful items in her periphery.

He caught her lips in a soft, sweet kiss. The backs of his fingers feathered the warm curls at the apex of her thighs. Gently, so gently he touched her, but it was enough to generate all sorts of fiery little responses. When she moaned again, it had nothing to do with the soreness.

Riding on the pleasure brought by his stroking fin-gers, she whispered his name, then said in the same awe-filled breath, "This could go on forever."

"Let it," he whispered back. His fingers sank deeper and he delighted in the audible catch in her breath.

"I've never been like this," came her soft words of de-nial, but her eyes were closed, her lips remained parted, and she'd bent one knee to give him better access.

He was up on an elbow, alternately watching her face and the action of his hand. His voice was thick. "It's good for you."

"So much?" she whispered.

"Uh-huh."

She gave a tiny gasp and undulated against his hand. "We have to stop . . ."

"Not yet."

"I don't know . . . how much more I can take."

"Just this."

Her fingers dug into his shoulders. "Brendan!" Her breathy cry held both surprise and wonder, which was incredible to Brendan, since he'd brought her to many other climaxes in the course of the night. But her body rocked under the force of this one, and by the time the spasms had begun to wane, she had her face buried in the crook of his shoulder.

In time she let out a long, ragged breath.

"Good?" he whispered huskily.

"Mmm."

They lay for several minutes listening to the gentle sough of the warm rain falling in the courtyard and, beyond that, the distant sounds of traffic.

"Whatever must you think of me?" she murmured, raising sheepish eyes to his.

"I think," he said, "that you're a very passionate woman."

Her hand was resting on his stomach. She slid it lower, whispering, "And you? You share the passion. Will you let me pleasure you, too?"

His fingers closed around hers, guiding them back the way they'd come. "Not now." He kissed her forehead.

"But you're hard—"

"And enjoying the knowledge that I've satisfied you. It's enough this time."

Caroline found it hard to believe that a man could be so selfless. Yet, studying his face, she saw nothing but sincerity etched in his features. "Are you sure?" she asked in a whisper.

He smiled and nodded.

What a handsome smile, she thought. A confident smile. A gentle and generous one. It caused a distinct tightening in the region of her heart.

To counter that tightening, she sent him an accusing look. "You've bewitched me, I think. Either that or there's something in the air. Do you suppose exhaust fumes from the courtyard could be an aphrodisiac?"

Barely restraining a grin, he shook his head.

Her grunt held begrudging agreement. She didn't smell exhaust fumes; she never had. At the moment, though, the air surrounding them was musty, a mixture of humidity, sleep and sex that she found to be delightfully earthy.

Closing her eyes, she fit herself more snugly into the arm Brendan offered and smiled in contentment when he began to stroke her hair. It amazed her that she welcomed the physical contact, particularly given the weather. But then, physical contact with Brendan was like nothing she'd ever known before. It was new and refreshing, offering a counterpoint to the heat. His firm body supported hers even as it yielded to her curves. Regardless of how casual or incidental, his touch was exciting in the tremors it caused, and in the case of deliberate provocation it was stimulating, sensual and satisfying. It was also a total distraction from the rest of the world.

Body and mind, both buzzed with lingering pleasure. Caroline was thinking that she could spend the entire day with him this way when he gently eased her aside and rose from the bed.

Bending down to kiss the tip of her nose, he whispered, "Be right back," before disappearing into the bathroom. When he reemerged moments later, he crossed to the refrigerator, poured a large glass of orange juice and delivered it to her in the bed.

"I'm impressed," she said, propping a pillow between her back and the headboard. She accepted the orange juice, took a healthy drink, then handed it back. "Breakfast in bed. Not bad."

He took a swallow of juice. "If I were truly chivalrous, I'd be making an exotic omelet."

"It's okay. I'm not a breakfast person." She smirked. "But you don't know that, do you?"

Pursing his lips, he shook his head slowly. "Can't see in during the day. I only know you as a creature of the night."

She chuckled at that. "You make me sound wicked."

"Not wicked. Maybe wild or sensual, even wanton, but never wicked." He slid down against the headboard until they were flush side to side and slanted her a glance. "So. Since we've blown a trip to Maine, what's your pleasure? Washington is a romantic city. We could play tourist and walk around in the rain."

"In the rain?" she echoed meaningfully.

"Mmm. Forget walking around. We could take a drive to the country."

She considered that, but again there was the rain and somehow the thought of being restrained for hours in a car with Brendan's hands stuck on the wheel bothered her. She crinkled her nose in rejection of the idea.

"I could leave you in peace," he suggested cautiously. "You could do whatever you'd do on a normal Saturday—" She interrupted him with a vigorous shake of her head. Relieved, he spread his arms in a gesture of self-sacrifice. "I'm at your disposal. You name it."

What she really wanted to do was to stay right there all day. She felt pleasantly tired and thoroughly sated. Her body's soreness would respond to a warm bath, and she rather liked the idea of taking one with Brendan, then just lying around talking, making love, thumbing her nose at the busy pace of the rest of her life.

But, Lord, what would he think if she suggested a full day of lazing around? He might revise his assessment of her to wicked after all. What she needed, she decided, was for *him* to suggest that they idle away the day together.

The phone rang just then. She shot a glance in its direction, then returned her gaze to Brendan. When the second ring came, she plopped a wet kiss on the tiny white scar on the tip of his chin, climbed over his body and padded across the floor to the peninsula. She had the instrument halfway to her ear before she thought twice, but by then it was too late.

"Hello?"

"What's going on, Caroline? I got a call from Elliot a few minutes ago. He's furious."

"Norman," she breathed, looking distinctly regretful as she turned around to face Brendan. If only she'd stopped to think before she'd picked up the phone. If only she'd let the damned thing ring. If only she'd put on her machine. "How're ya doin', Norman?" she asked conversationally.

"Not real well, considering that my brother just ruined the peace of my Saturday brunch."

She felt a surge of guilt. "I'm sorry," she said on impulse, then added, "He shouldn't have done that."

"What I want to know is why he did. What happened between you two?"

Caroline's eyes were on Brendan, who was lounging against the headboard with one knee bent and an arm folded behind his head. She had his full attention, which, thank heavens, wasn't a problem. He knew about Elliot. He knew about Elliot's relationship to Norman. And the sight of him—his mere presence—calmed her.

"What did he say?" she asked quietly.

"He said you'd been two-timing him."

"He's upset."

"He said you'd been using him."

She felt another twinge of guilt. True, she'd used Elliot as a buffer between Ben and her, but Elliot knew nothing of that. As for the accusations he'd made the evening before—accusations she was sure he'd repeated to his brother—she was innocent.

"He's misinterpreted things, Norman."

"So, what's the story?"

She shook her head in dismay. "I can't believe he called you."

"He's my brother. My *younger* brother."

"But he's still thirty-six," she argued, tamping down a spurt of annoyance. "Did he really expect that you'd come running to his rescue and make everything all right?"

"I'm not sure what he expected. Maybe he just had to let off steam. But if I can help him, I'd like to."

Caroline gave a tiny sigh. Norman was a good guy. For that matter, so was Elliot. Between them, though, they were going about things the wrong way. "I'd like to help him, too," she said, "which is why I was going to call him later."

"He seems to feel that it's over between you."

"It is."

"Because of another man?"

She felt another little burst of annoyance and had to remind herself that this was Norman, her partner. If she lashed out and antagonized him, things would be uncomfortable at work. Besides, she really did like him. While he had no business prying into her personal life, his heart was in the right place.

"No," she answered calmly. "It's over because of Elliot and me. We're not right for a long-term relationship."

"I thought you were perfect for each other."

"Oh, Norman," she said with a sad smile and a sigh. "You *wanted* us to be perfect for each other."

"Sure I did. He's my brother and you're my partner and I like you both. What could have been nicer?"

"'Nice' doesn't necessarily make for a good marriage."

"You know what I mean."

"Yes."

"Were you really planning on calling him?"

"Yes."

"Please do, Caroline. I think you owe it to him."

"I know that, Norman."

"I've never heard him so angry."

"His pride is hurt."

Norman hesitated for an instant, clearly trying to be diplomatic about something he'd already mentioned once but unable to restrain his curiosity. "He did say something about another man."

She gnawed on her lower lip. What she had with Brendan was private. Still, she wondered if a touch of the truth wouldn't go a long way toward pacifying Norman.

Her lip slid free of her teeth. "Elliot asked me out for this weekend and I refused. In spite of that, he showed up last night. While he was here, a friend of mine—a neighbor—arrived."

"A man?"

"Yes."

"Are you dating him?"

"I hadn't been before last night, but now, yes, I think so."

"So Elliot saw you with the guy, after you'd turned down a date with him."

"Elliot was in my apartment uninvited when he saw my neighbor arrive," she argued. "To tell you the truth, I was grateful my neighbor appeared. Elliot was being a little pushy."

"Pushy? What do you mean?"

"I think you know," she murmured, quickly regretting she'd mentioned it. "Listen, Norman, all I can say is that I will call Elliot. If you want to know anything more, you really ought to ask him."

"He's apt to tell me to take a flying leap."

She snickered softly. "Why didn't *I* think of that?"

"Because you're too diplomatic. You really would be good for Elliot, you know. You'd tone him down—"

"Norman . . ."

"Okay. Go back to whatever it was you were doing. I'll talk with you later. Bye-bye."

Very quietly, she replaced the phone in its cradle. Averting her eyes from Brendan, she set to work putting a pot of coffee on to drip. "He told me to go back to whatever it was I was doing," she said self-consciously. "He should only know."

Brendan had easily gotten the gist of the phone conversation. He was wondering whether this unwelcome intrusion from the outside world would sour her on their relationship. "How do you feel?"

"About what we've been doing?" She indulged in a private smile. "Perfectly justified and content."

"How do you feel about Norman's call?"

The smile faded. "Badly. It was enough that Elliot was upset. Now he's upset Norman, so things are worse." Setting down the coffee canister, she turned pleading eyes to Brendan. "Why did he do that? Why did he have to call his brother right off the bat to complain?"

"Maybe he just needed to talk to someone."

She considered that for a moment, then gave a negligent shrug.

Brendan tried again. "Maybe he thought that Norman could straighten you out."

She gave a soft snort, but she supposed that possibility was real.

He regarded her more soberly. "Maybe he wanted to beat you to the punch. Maybe he was afraid you'd get to Norman first with a report of attempted assault."

She had to admit that that did make sense. She hadn't thought of what Elliot had done as an attempted assault, since she'd handled it and emerged without a bruise. But a court of law certainly might see things differently. Perhaps Elliot realized that. "It wasn't really...so bad," she said in Elliot's defense. And I pretty much did tell Norman about it."

"Only at his goading. At least, I assume he was goading."

"Yes."

She'd turned back to the coffee when Brendan rose from the bed and came to her side. "Don't let it get you down. You handled Norman well, and you'll do the same with Elliot."

"Why do I feel like such a crumb?"

"Because you've conditioned yourself to feel that way." He tipped his head and gave her a humorous once-over. "You don't *look* like a crumb. Do you realize that you're parading around here stark naked, without a stitch of clothing, much less modesty?"

She returned the once-over indulgently. "Look who's talking."

"Isn't it great?" he asked with such a boyish grin that she had to shake her head in chiding.

"You are impossible. Here I am, trying to grapple with a serious dilemma, and your mind is in the gutter."

He hooked an arm around her waist and anchored her to his side. "The gutter? No way! I'm simply saying that we're perfectly at ease with each other, and isn't that nice? Besides," he rushed on, "I think you have to put your 'serious dilemma' in perspective. Norman knows about what's happened. You were dreading his finding out, but that's over and done now. He's been mollified, hasn't he? And you've already made the decision to call Elliot. So, what's to grapple with—other than deciding what you want to do today?"

Before Caroline could answer, the phone rang again. This time she did think twice. After another ring and continued indecision on her part, Brendan lifted the receiver and put it to her ear.

She offered a hesitant "Hello?"

"It's me. Did you speak to Diane?" The accusation in Carl's voice left no doubt that his question wasn't idle.

She mouthed, "my brother," to Brendan before speaking into the phone. "We had dinner together last week, but I already told you about that. She's called several times since then. Why? What's happened?"

"She informed me that I was being impulsive and that, according to you, if she gave me a little time I'd come to my senses."

Caroline closed her eyes and slowly shook her head. She wasn't denying what Carl said, simply trying to understand how her good friend Diane could have been so tactless as to repeat her advice verbatim and then quote the source.

With a squeeze to her shoulder, Brendan left her side. She opened her eyes to watch him as he finished making the coffee. The sight of him gave her resolve.

"It's true, Carl. You are being impulsive."

"Since when are you the authority?"

She was careful to keep her voice gentle, though she had no intention of backing down. "Since we were kids and you dumped every little problem in my lap. Since I was an undergraduate psychology major. Since I earned a Ph.D. in counseling."

At the last bit of news, Brendan's brows went up. Caroline waved away the significance of the degree with her hand.

Carl was equally unimpressed. "Don't throw fancy qualifications at me. I'm not your client."

"Right. You're my brother, which means that I know you better than I know most of my clients. You've always been impulsive. Things get a little rocky between you and Diane and you throw up your hands and decide that that's it, it's over. You move out of the house and start divorce proceedings without ever sitting down and trying to talk things through with her."

"She's making crazy demands."

"Do you have any idea why? Because she's trying to shock you into slowing down and thinking, really thinking, about all this. She doesn't want a divorce, Carl. She loves you."

"Oh, yeah."

"She does."

"Then she has a strange way of showing it."

The coffee started to drip. Brendan paused in his hunt for the mugs to give her an encouraging wink.

Caroline didn't take her eyes from him. "You've backed her into a corner. Maybe if you offer her a hand, she'll be able to express herself better."

"Offer her a hand," Carl retorted, "and she'd take both, and where would that leave me?"

"Happily married?"

"Fat chance."

Dropping her gaze to the floor, she sighed. "Look, Carl, you have to do something. I've suggested marital counseling, but you've vetoed that idea more than once. You and Diane have to talk. If you don't you'll find yourself all alone down the road."

"You're on her side."

"I'm not on anyone's side."

"Bullshit."

"No, Carl." Her patience was beginning to wear thin. "I'm rooting for you and Diane as a couple. You have so much going for yourselves. Take my word for it, your problems are minor compared to some that couples work through."

With a vocal growl of frustration, Carl hung up the phone.

Caroline stared at the silent receiver for several long moments before slowly replacing it. She stood with her fingers curled around the edge of the counter and her head bowed. "I feel useless. Nothing I say seems to help, which would be fine if they didn't keep dragging me into it."

Brendan reached over and tucked a wayward lock of hair behind her ear. "You've tried. What more can they ask?"

"Nothing, I suppose. But, damn, it's a little like the teacher whose own kid is flunking out of school. My field is counseling, but when it comes to the marriage of my brother and my best friend, I might as well be a . . . a caterer."

He laughed. "Where'd that come from?"

A crooked smile stole to her lips. "It's my secret ambition. I've never been able to cook for beans."

"I take it that's a warning."

"Uh-huh." Her eyes had grown teasing as they clung to his. She didn't want to brood. She couldn't possibly brood—not with Brendan here. He lifted her spirits, removing the weight that would otherwise have dragged them down. Yes, she felt badly about the call from Carl, but she felt something else. She felt like a person. Brendan's presence was a reminder that she had a right to her own life. "You're good to put up with all this," she said in thanks.

"All what?" Brendan asked. He had been momentarily distracted by that look in her eye and had been thinking that she could make him feel like a million without uttering a word.

"My phone calls. Another man would have had his pants on long before Norman had finished."

He shifted those marvelous shoulders of his. "I like being naked."

She shot a glance toward the window and tempered a grin. "Lucky for us it's daylight. Who knows what that

pervert across the courtyard would make of our danc-
ing around in the nude."

"Since I'm 'that pervert' and I'm here, not there, I give
us permission." He drew her into a snug embrace, took
a long, deep breath and gave a loud sigh of satisfaction.
"This is what I like."

She nodded her agreement against his chest, then
opened her mouth to tell him what she'd really like to do
all day when the phone rang again. Instead of speaking,
she gave a growl much like the frustrated one Carl had
made before he'd hung up.

"Does this happen every Saturday?" Brendan asked.

"Yeah. Let's go to your place."

"My place is a mess."

The phone rang again.

"But at least it's peaceful," she argued in a higher voice
than usual. "That has to be either my mother or my sister."

"You're not the only one who has 'em," he drawled.

She held him back and looked up. "Uh-oh. You get
calls, too?"

The phone rang the third time. Scowling, she reached
over, snatched it up and would have bellowed into it had
Brendan not put a timely thumb against her lips. Very
slowly he drew the thumb away. Very sweetly she said,
"Hello?"

"Hi, Caro. I'm not in labor, but let me tell you, I have
a pain in the butt! Mom is driving me nuts! She called me
two minutes ago babbling on and on about a malprac-
tice suit, and it's not the first time she's mentioned it. But
it's so *pointless* for her to go on about it when she doesn't
even know how much of a case she has. She has to wait
to see how dad's leg heals. Do you think she's asked him
how he would feel about a lawsuit? He probably wants

no part of it. She has no *idea* what a suit like that will entail. She'll have to hire a lawyer—I told her *I* couldn't do it—and go through the hassle of collecting evidence, not to mention putting Dad through more and more exams. It'll take tons of time, a load of money and the case could piddle around in the courts for years. By the time she's done, they'll put *her* on the stand and prove she's loony!''

Since Caroline hadn't been able to get a word in, she'd shifted the phone away from her mouth and was filling Brendan in on the side.

Somehow, between her own words, Karen managed to overhear the low murmurs. ''Who's there?''

''A friend,'' Caroline answered, giving her sister the perfect opening to apologize for interrupting and say she'd call back later.

Karen did neither. After a short and distracted ''Oh,'' she barreled on. ''You have to help me, Caro. Get her off my back. I can't take her paranoid nonsense on top of everything else that's happening.''

''There's not much I can do.''

''Call her. Let her babble away to *you*.''

''Thanks a lot,'' Caroline mumbled. If Karen heard, she ignored the sarcasm.

''You have so much more patience, Caro!''

''And you're the lawyer. You have the credence. I've told Mom that she'd be foolish to think of suing right now, but she won't listen to me. I've tried, really I have.'' Gratefully, she accepted the cup of coffee Brendan pressed into her hand, then shook her head when he made a stirring motion with his finger, silently asking if she wanted cream or sugar.

''Try again!'' Karen ordered on a slightly hysterical note.

"Karen, calm down. If she's already called you today, you're off the hook for a while."

"For a day."

"No doubt she'll be calling me, and when she does, I'll do my best to divert her."

"Just tell her to leave me alone."

"I can't do that."

"Sure you can, if you do it nicely."

"I have a better idea, Karen. Why don't you let Dan answer the phone and say that you're working or shopping or sleeping?"

For the first time Karen paused. "I hate to put the burden on Dan."

*What about the burden you're putting on me?* Caroline asked silently. Aloud she said, "Dan can handle it."

"I'll tell him you said so. Oops, there he is. I've got to run, Caro. He'll be loaded down with grocery bags. I'll call you later. Bye." She was already yelling, "Coming, sweetheart," before she'd hung up the phone.

Caroline hung up on her own end and, turning to Brendan, rolled her eyes in frustration. "She's incredible! She knew someone was here, yet she babbled on and on about Mom's babbling." The phone rang. Her voice dropped to a low, stiff monotone. "That's Mom. Don't touch it."

"She'll keep trying. Why not get it out of the way?"

Squeezing her eyes shut, Caroline pressed her fingertips to her forehead. It was an instinctive gesture, made in anticipation of the headache she was sure to get if she spoke with her mother."

Since she wasn't looking, Brendan picked up the phone. His deep voice rang out with just the right amount of deference. "Cooper residence."

Caroline spread her fingers and dragged them downward, peering through the cracks at Brendan. His grin was a dead giveaway of her mother's startled sputter at the other end of the line. With little effort, Caroline could imagine her mother's words.

*Who is this?*

"This is Brendan Carr."

*Who is that?*

"I'm a friend of Caroline's."

*What are you doing there?*

"Visiting."

*At this hour?*

He squinted back at the clock. "It's nearly noon." Winking at Caroline, he asked innocently, "Who is this?" Caroline could just imagine the tone in which her mother informed him of her identity. "Ahh. Mrs. Cooper. How are you?"

It was the wrong thing to ask. Caroline knew it the instant the words left Brendan's mouth. She stood back and watched while he listened to a prolonged monologue, no doubt about Madeline Cooper's raw nerves, her husband's broken leg and the weather, in that order.

Brendan shifted from one foot to the other. He hooked his hand on his hip, alternately nodding in silent sympathy for Madeline and ogling various parts of Caroline's body. It was all Caroline could do not to laugh aloud at the abrupt switches.

At some point, though, the direction of Madeline's talk changed, because he said a bit defensively, "I was next to the phone. It made sense for me to answer."

Picturing her mother getting huffy, Caroline reached for the phone. She got Brendan's hand instead, long fingers threading through hers, curving around them, holding firm.

"Her hands are tied up at the moment," he dared say when Madeline asked to speak with Caroline. "Perhaps she could get back to you."

Caroline tried to free her hand without success, so she reached for the phone with the other one. Brendan simply turned to render the instrument beyond reach. In doing so, he brought their bodies into contact. Caroline stopped struggling.

"She won't be here then," Brendan was saying. "We're just getting ready to leave." Caroline arched a single curious brow, but he was a step ahead of her. "We thought we'd take a drive down to—" He was interrupted. "I know that she doesn't have a car. I have one." He stopped again. "It's a Toyota. Very safe. And I'm a good driver. I have never had an accident in—" He broke off for a minute while Madeline talked. "Please, Mrs. Cooper, there's no need to be superstitious. I'm not 'due' for an accident. I have a perfect record because I'm careful."

Caroline was enjoying herself. She'd offered to take the phone; Brendan had refused. Now he was seeing first-hand what it was about Madeline Cooper that could drive a sane soul mad.

"The drivers are no worse here than anywhere else," he pointed out patiently, then said a minute later, "I'm sure you're right, in terms of expense if nothing else. If Caroline doesn't need a car, it's pointless for her to have one." He listened to something Madeline said, then blinked. "I suppose you could say that we're dating."

Had he been wearing a shirt, he would have been growing hot under the collar. Caroline could see that his pleasant expression was more forced with each of Madeline's questions. She would have felt sorry for him had he not asked for the torture himself.

"Fairly recently," he said. Then, "Yes." After a longer pause, he looked at Caroline. "My intentions?"

Caroline's smug grin disappeared. "Oh, no," she whispered plaintively, "she can't ask that!"

"We've only just begun to date," Brendan reminded Madeline. "It's a little early to discuss . . . of course I'm an honorable man. I wouldn't do a thing...you shouldn't be worrying about that."

When Madeline jabbered on, he took the phone from his ear and belatedly offered it to Caroline, who opened her eyes wide in an are-you-kidding look and shook her head. Reluctantly he returned the phone to his ear.

"Uh-huh . . . of course I understand . . . would it be possible for her to call you Monday?" He shut his eyes briefly at whatever it was Madeline said. "No, Mrs. Cooper, that's not so . . . no, I am not trying to keep you from talking to her . . . excuse me? Holding her prisoner?" Wearing a look of utter incredulity, he murmured to Caroline, "Tied up and gagged?" Clearing his throat, he returned to Madeline. "Please, Mrs. Cooper, if you'll hold on a minute, I'll see if Caroline can come to the phone."

Exasperated, he thrust the receiver at Caroline.

*I warned you,* her eyes said.

His answered, *Next time I'll listen.*

Caroline spent the next several minutes assuring her mother that she was well, happy and free. No sooner had that been accomplished than Madeline wanted to know—from Caroline's lips, despite the fact that Brendan had already given her much of the same information—who Brendan was, where he lived, how she'd met him, how long she'd been seeing him and what he did for a living. Caroline's answers varied from straightforward to evasive. She kept them brief. She did *not* ask how her mother was, instead repeating what Brendan had said about getting ready to leave. After promising to call at the start of the week, she hung up the phone.

Brendan instantly snatched it up, punched out information, then, with his eyes glued to Caroline's, asked for the number of the Canterbury Hotel. Moments later, he had reserved a suite for the night.

Caroline hadn't said a word. She was watching the expressions that crossed his face, expressions ranging from frustration to determination to desire. Now there was caution.

"Is that okay with you?" he asked. His hand remained on the telephone receiver. He would cancel the reservations in an instant if she had qualms.

Caroline had no qualms whatsoever. The Canterbury was reputed to be one of the most charming hotels in Washington. Though she'd never seen it herself, she'd been told about the classical music in the lobby and the period furnishings in the rooms. It would be cool and comfortable and quiet. She could laze around with Brendan to her heart's content.

A smile tugged at the corner of her mouth. "No one will know we're there."

He slid an arm around her waist. "That's the idea."

"I like it. What should I bring?"

"Not much. We could dress up for dinner if you want."

"I'm sure they have room service."

"Uh-huh."

"Have you ever done this before?"

"Nope." His eyes had grown darker, more luminous. "It's been a fantasy, though, and since we're into living out fantasies . . ."

Very gently, almost hypnotically, he reached for her. Her arms quite naturally looped around his neck. Her flesh met his with the same ease but with excitement, as well. It was incredible, she realized, the ease and the excitement—incredible and unique. But then, wasn't that what a fantasy was all about?

# 8

THE TWENTY-FOUR HOURS that Caroline and Brendan
spent at the Canterbury were heavenly. They didn't leave
their room during that time, and not once were they
bored. They made love, slept and talked about most
anything that came to mind. When they felt the need for
food, they called room service.

Caroline surprised herself. She'd been exhausted all
week; her dream cure should have been a restful and
companionable silence. But with Brendan she wanted to
talk. He fascinated her—his background, his life-style,
his work. She devoted herself to feeding that fascination. And when he asked her questions in return, she
found that she could tell him anything.

She did call in early Sunday morning for an auto-
matic playback of the messages on her answering machine. She told Brendan she wanted to know that her
sister was all right, but they both knew it was something
more. No one knew where they were. Caroline didn't
miss the nagging phone calls, but she couldn't shake the
fear that if something did happen to one of the family, no
one would be able to contact her and therefore she'd be
unable to help.

It was a catch-22. She wouldn't have had to worry if
she'd left Karen or Carl the number where she could be
reached in an emergency. But if she'd done that, she'd
have opened herself to unnecessary calls—precisely what
she was trying to escape.

With Caroline, responsibility was a habit of long standing. Brendan understood that. He couldn't equate it with a habit like smoking, because it was neither life-threatening nor undesirable. A sense of responsibility was a good thing to have—unless it became a detriment to one's own peace of mind, in which case it had to be put in perspective. That was what Caroline was going to have to learn how to do.

In the meantime, Brendan could be patient. He knew that she couldn't just snap her fingers and, presto, set aside all family concerns. He wouldn't have wanted her to. It would have been out of character, and he was finding that he adored her character. She was proving to be the kindest, most interesting and uninhibited woman he'd ever met.

He wondered whether she was this way with everyone—talking freely, asking questions, sometimes doing the opposite and listening so quietly that he was convinced he was boring her to tears, only to have her come back with an insightful, thoughtfully presented response that forwarded the discussion, often lifting it to a higher plane. He felt intellectually challenged. By virtue of the questions she asked or the comments she made, he was thinking about things in ways that he hadn't done before. He felt productive.

Selfishly, he wanted to think that she was this way only with him. He wanted to think that, even beyond their agreement, he offered her something that she'd previously been without. The key, if it was true, was in making her see it.

While not thinking quite as far down the road, Caroline couldn't remember a time when she'd felt so free of the burdens of the world, and she said as much to Brendan as they gathered together their single, embarrassingly light bag of possessions and prepared to check out of the hotel early Sunday afternoon. "I'd like to stay here forever."

"No, you wouldn't," he countered only half in jest. "You'd get itchy to be up and out and around in the world."

Wrapping her arms around his waist, she turned her face up to his. "Are you?"

"No."

"Then why should I be?"

"Because you said you wanted freedom. You want to come and go as you please. No strings. No restrictions. No hassles."

"In a manner of speaking, I've had all of that here. It's been idyllic. Maybe that's why I want to stay." The thought of returning to the real world was making her feel a little blue.

Brendan didn't want to push his luck by exploring her feelings more deeply than, in fact, she was ready to do herself. So he said, "I guess we both needed a vacation."

"It's more than that. We didn't get away, but we...got away." She crinkled up her nose. "Do you know what I mean?"

"You bet."

"I wish we'd had more time."

"We can always come again."

"I'd like that," she said with a soft smile and a resurgence of enthusiasm.

Brendan felt his breath catch in his throat. The soul touch of her eyes did that to him. Add to it the softness of her smile and he was a goner.

Several minutes passed before he was able to respond, and then his voice had a gruff edge to it. "You're too agreeable, Caroline. I can see how you get yourself involved in doing things you don't really want to do."

"But I *would* like to come here again, or go to another place like this. Maybe we could try an inn in the country next time. I have a terrific book that lists them."

"You're a fan of country inns?"

"I like reading about them."

"Have you visited many?"

She shook her head. "I daydream a lot."

"Why only daydream?"

"Because," she answered without pretense, "it's no fun to travel alone."

Something warm and reassuring flowed through Brendan just then. It was his life's blood, he knew, but it was infused with new vigor. He felt suddenly stronger, more buoyant. He felt as though the future was definitely looking bright.

THE FEELING LASTED for six hours. During that time he and Caroline ambled slowly through Georgetown, pausing to browse in the shops or eat or find a comfortable spot to sit and talk. At the end, though, they reached her door. She invited him in, but he had to return to his loft to organize his papers and thoughts before his trip the next morning. When he invited her back to his place to read or relax while he worked, she smiled—a little sadly, he thought—and said that she'd better catch up on her own chores. So they kissed with a brief, sweet passion and parted.

In hindsight, Brendan realized that they'd been foolish in not choosing one of their lofts and staying together. He didn't get much done that evening. He tried, but his gaze regularly wandered through the open French windows and across the courtyard. Whenever he caught

Caroline's eye, he went to the window and indulged in that special, silent communication they shared.

The game they were playing was a torturous one. The night was humid, and he was hot in every sense of the word. Kneeling on her window seat, with her hair caught at the top of her head, the skin of her face and neck visibly moist, her thin shift simultaneously covering everything and nothing, Caroline was even more the innocent seductress than she'd been before. Because now he knew her. Now there were open smiles and meaningful gestures. He knew what it felt like to plow his fingers into her hair, to catch trickles of sweat with his tongue, to explore the feminine curves beneath her shift. She had merely to rest her head against the window frame or scoop loose strands of hair from her neck or arch her back in a hot, lazy stretch and he was on fire. Everything about her was simply sultry.

But she was there and he was here and because of that he felt uneasy. He cursed the timing that was engineering a separation so early in their relationship. He had no doubts about his feelings for her. After weeks of daydreaming, he'd only had to meet her briefly to know that she was the woman for him. But he needed more time to convince *her*.

He knew that she felt something for him. What they'd experienced that weekend had gone far beyond the sexual marathon they'd joked about. If it had been only sex, they'd never have been able to talk as they'd done. And there was something else—he had to smile a little slyly when he thought of it—something that was promising. Caroline had insisted on taking his spare key so that she could drop his mail in his apartment each day. He'd made vague sounds of protest, but she'd said that she really wanted to do it, that it was something she'd do for any good friend and certainly she considered him that. He refrained from pointing out that "doing things" was what she'd wanted to avoid. He suspected that she truly did enjoy being generous with her time and effort—when she didn't feel taken for granted. And he took care to see that she didn't.

The fact of the matter was that he liked knowing she'd be checking into his loft each day. It was a small thing, a link, and it gave him solace at a time when he was needy.

His greatest fear—it came to him in cold flicks of emptiness—was that someone else would discover her and steal her away while he was gone. He knew he was being silly, because while he was gone she'd be going to work, seeing the same people she always saw, and if nothing had clicked with any of those people before, there was no logical reason why it would now. But it seemed incredible to him that she *hadn't* been discovered before. She was so perfect. Didn't the rest of the world see it?

Four days. That was all he'd be gone. But, damn, he wished he weren't going at all.

His greatest frustration, he decided, was that he couldn't share his greatest fear with her. If he'd had his way, he'd have already bared his heart and begged a commitment. But that wasn't part of the bargain he'd made with her—which was also why he'd been evasive when Mrs. Cooper had asked about his intentions toward her daughter.

Intentions seemed an old-fashioned word to him, and he'd never thought of himself as an old-fashioned man, yet what he felt for Caroline was old-fashioned through and through. He wanted the whole thing—flowers, double rings, the wedding march, the bridal suite—and he wanted it yesterday.

But he'd wait. He'd wait until Caroline acknowledged what he already had—that along the line of their unorthodox introduction, what they shared was totally and wonderfully unique. He'd wait if it killed him—not that he'd be twiddling his thumbs in the interim. He'd work on her subtly but steadily. She wouldn't know what had hit her until she was well and truly hooked.

CAROLINE KNEW very well what had hit her. She couldn't deny that when she went to work Monday morning her spirits were soaring. To some extent, she was feeling relief. She'd called Elliot the night before, and though he'd been miserly with words himself, she felt that she'd explained herself well and smoothed over at least one or two raw edges.

In greater part, though, her light spirits were due to Brendan. For the first time in her life, she had an ally. He was someone to talk with and play with. He'd proven himself capable of listening and offering compassion and advice. He'd even taken on her mother—something that they'd laughed about afterward but that had meant the world to her. A little help, a breather once in a while— that was all she asked. And Brendan seemed more than willing to provide it. He'd told her to use him. She didn't even have to feel guilty when she did it.

So, life seemed a little easier. The knowledge that she'd be talking to Brendan, then seeing him later in the week was the touchstone she needed when those little frustrations piled up. And they did that.

When he phoned on Monday night and asked about her day, she readily told him about her mother's call. "The phone rang at seven o'clock this morning, Brendan. That's six o'clock her time, and mother's never been a naturally early riser. She was probably counting the hours all weekend."

"What did she have to say?" Brendan asked. He had a good idea what the answer was, but he wasn't about to offer a guess when he knew that Caroline needed to let off steam by relating it all herself. Besides, he took pleasure in hearing her voice.

"She wanted to know where we went this weekend, what we did and what time we got back."

"Did you tell her?"

"I told her what time we got back."

"She wasn't satisfied with just that, was she?"

"No. I kind of fudged the rest."

"You could have told her the truth."

"Are you kidding? And open up a whole other can of worms?"

Brendan chuckled. "She doesn't actually think you're still a virgin, does she?"

"She pretends I am. I told her that particular truth quite bluntly years ago, but she chose not to hear, and it's occurred to me since that I'd be wise not to press the point. Do you have any idea what would have happened if I'd told her what we really did this weekend?"

"What?"

"AIDS. She could have gone on and on about AIDS."

"Oh, no."

"Oh, yes. She would have asked how well I really knew you and did I know whether you'd had many women before me and was I positively certain you weren't bisexual and giving me something that could well be fatal."

"Damn good thing I ruled it out at the start," he mumbled in a Lord-help-us tone. "Has she done that sort of thing before?"

"She's made general statements about every other sexually transmitted disease. She tells me about so-and-so who contracted such-and-such, and she babbles on for such a long time that I *know* there's a direct message in there for me."

"She must have known you were sleeping with Ben."

"She tried not to."

"Did she like him?"

"Like him?" Caroline echoed tongue-in-cheek. "How could she like him? She never got past the point of wondering whether he was a spy infiltrating the diplomatic corps on behalf of the KGB."

Brendan didn't want to think what the woman would say when she learned that he dealt with terrorism. "She really is an alarmist, isn't she?"

"Oh, yes. What bothers me most, I think, is that she should trust me to know what I'm doing and she doesn't." Caroline took a deep breath. She'd been annoyed all day by the call from her mother, but somehow, after telling Brendan about it, she felt better. Unburdened. A tiny smile played at the corners of her mouth. "By the way, she said that you had a nice voice."

"She did?" he asked, pleased with that.

"Uh-huh. She said that it was compelling in a gentle way—then she went on to warn me to be careful because men with low, charming voices weren't always to be trusted. She said that I should be on my guard, that you might try to con me into something."

He heard the smile in her voice. "Are you? On your guard, that is?"

"Sure am," she said, but the softness of her tone hinted that she wasn't terribly worried. She trusted him, which was one of the reasons why, when he called on Tuesday night and again asked about her day, she found herself telling him about Paul Valente.

She was disturbed by the meeting she'd had with Paul that day. Without mentioning names, she briefly filled Brendan in on the situation between Paul and his wife. "He canceled their appointment last week, and this week he came in alone to say that she'd left him. He was really down. I was a little surprised."

"That he was so upset?"

"No, no. I knew he'd be upset. I just didn't think he'd express it as openly as he did. Other than isolated minutes before or after a session, I've always counseled them together. He comes across very differently when he's with his wife. Alone, he's a more sympathetic character."

"It sounds like he got to you today."

"Yes. I feel really bad. He doesn't want this separation. He wants to work things out."

"Is there any chance of that?"

"Not unless he can somehow convince his wife to sit down and talk, but since communication has never been their strong suit as a couple, the chances of that are slim."

Brendan knew what she wasn't saying. He could hear it in her discouraged tone. "I think you're blaming yourself for not being able to do more."

"Yes," she said quietly.

"I'm sure you did what you could."

"It wasn't enough. You know," she went on plaintively, "it wouldn't be so bad if he'd have come to me and said that they were separating but that it was the best thing, that he felt relieved because they were really making each other miserable. In a situation like that, I've failed but I haven't. I can tell myself that therapy served a purpose in clarifying their relationship for them. I can look back on it as a last-ditch effort to save something that in the end neither partner cared enough to save. That might have been true for the wife in this case, but not for her husband. He does love her."

"So you feel that you've personally failed him," Brendan concluded with compassion. "But the burden of responsibility wasn't totally yours, Caroline. The fellow's *wife* failed him, because she reneged on certain vows she'd once made. She was the one who gave up on the marriage, not you."

His words soothed her. The plaintive quality had left her voice. "But maybe I could have prevented it," Caroline argued more calmly, then tacked on a bewildered "somehow."

"You tried your best, didn't you?"

"I thought I did at the time."

"Isn't that the bottom line?" he asked softly, then raised his voice a notch. "Hey, I know exactly what you're feeling. When I was a prosecutor in the D.A.'s office, there was many a case I lost despite weeks and weeks of preparation. I could be totally convinced, I mean convinced beyond a shadow of a doubt, that a person was guilty of the crime for which he was being tried, but if that jury found him not guilty, there wasn't a damn thing I could do about it."

"Did you ever question your own competence?"

"All the time. After I lost a case like that, I'd sit down and review everything. There was learning value in it. Sometimes something would come to me in hindsight— something I'd done or hadn't done that could have been pivotal. When I first started, I made some mistakes. But as time went on, the problem was more often in the evidence itself. In other words, the case as I'd been handed it was not quite strong enough to win that conviction." He paused for the briefest of breaths. "Maybe the analogy fits here. Maybe the case you were given by this couple just wasn't strong enough. Certainly, if you tried your best, no one can find fault. The fact that the husband came in to see you today shows that he doesn't hold you responsible for the separation."

Caroline was feeling better because he did have a point. "If you were in his situation, Brendan, what would *you* feel? Would you be angry at me?"

Brendan tried to answer as honestly as possible. He respected Caroline too much to do any differently, and he wanted her respect, as well. Telling her only what he thought she wanted to hear would be counterproductive in that sense.

"Yes, I'd be angry, but only at first. I'd need to blame someone, and you'd be there. But when I stopped to think rationally, the anger would fade. I'd realize that I couldn't blame you for something you didn't create. Hell, you don't enter the picture of a relationship until it's in a shambles. Through the course of therapy, you can point out what's wrong, which I presume you did in this case. You can make suggestions for improving things, which I presume you did, also. You can even try to put those suggestions into effect during your sessions, but when you have only one hour a week to do it—" he exhaled a loud breath "—the odds have to be against you in those tough cases."

"It doesn't seem fair," Caroline concluded quietly.

"Life isn't, that way."

Those words were to echo in her mind the next day. When she spoke with Brendan on Wednesday night, she was particularly discouraged. "Karen called this morning in a panic. Her doctor has ordered her to bed until the baby is born."

"To bed? What happened?"

"She started bleeding. It doesn't have to do with the baby directly, but if she stays on her feet she's apt to bring on premature labor."

"When is she due?"

"That's one of the problems. The doctor says that she has another eight weeks to go, but she's convinced she conceived a month earlier. I'd almost agree with her. She's huge. She's been so uncomfortable for so long that we've been expecting the baby momentarily."

"Don't they have tests to determine that kind of thing?" he asked. He wished he knew more about the subject. Unfortunately, he was a virgin when it came to pregnancy and babies—not that he wasn't eager to learn, but eagerness alone couldn't provide the facts with which to offer Caroline comfort.

Caroline was every bit as naive. "Your asking me is like the blind leading the blind. I asked Karen the same question. She said something about an ultrasound test—that produces a picture of the baby. From the size of the skull they can tell the stage of gestation but only working up to a certain point in the pregnancy, after which it determines nothing more than the size of that particular baby. Anyway," she said with a sigh, "Karen didn't think to have the test done in time."

"Oh. Poor kid."

"The baby?"

"Karen. It won't help if she panics now."

"That's what I told her, too. But she really is distraught. She was planning to work right up to the end. Now she'll have to miss that many more weeks. She's convinced that she's blown a partnership."

"Nah. I can't believe that."

"Me, neither, but she does."

That he could believe. "Firms foster that kind of paranoia. They hold partnerships as the be-all and end-all, the carrot dangling in front of the associates' noses. You don't bring in enough cases, you don't get a partnership. You don't bill enough hours, you don't get a partnership. You alienate one of the partners, you don't get a partnership. They seem to think it increases productivity, when in the end it only fosters resentment and ill will."

"You sound happy to be away from it."

"Very. Large firms today are more like businesses than the professional institutions they used to be. Let me tell you, if Karen's firm denies or even withholds her partnership simply because of maternity matters, she could sue them for discrimination."

"What a pain."

"Mmm. If her firm does that, she'd be just as well free of it."

"The problem is that she doesn't want to be free of it. She's worked so hard to get where she is, and when it came to this pregnancy, she desperately wanted everything to work out. To have something like this happen . . . something she has no control over . . . she feels thwarted and very frustrated . . . I feel so bad for her, Brendan!"

"I know you do," he said gently, then added, "Hey, maybe you could visit her this weekend. That would probably calm her down . . . or perk her up . . . or whatever she needs by then."

Caroline had thought of that. It had been one of the first things to come to mind after Karen had told her the problem, and she'd barely kept herself from blurting out the offer. But she'd held her tongue. She didn't want to go to Karen's for the weekend. Not this weekend.

"I could do that," she said quietly.

Brendan heard her hesitance and, regardless of its cause, was pleased. He didn't want her spending the weekend with her sister. He wanted her spending the weekend with him.

Still, he knew that she'd be torn.

On the other hand, there was one way to satisfy them both. "How about I drive you up there?" he asked, then went quickly on. The plan was formulating fast, and he liked it. "Philly isn't so far. We could leave early Saturday morning, which would give you plenty of time to visit with Karen and Dan. After that we could drive just a little farther to one of those special inns you have in your book and spend the night, then return to see Karen again on Sunday before we head back here."

It was a super idea, if he did say so himself, and he couldn't help but smile in a self-satisfied, smugly male sort of way. But the smile faded quickly as it occurred to him that there was possibly one small flaw to his plan.

Caroline might not be ready to introduce him to her sister.

"Actually," he rushed on in the hope of compensating for that flaw, "I have friends in Philly myself. If you preferred, I could drop you at your sister's Saturday and pick you up there on Sunday. My friends have been nagging me to visit for months, so if you'd rather be alone with Karen, I could certainly understand."

"Brendan—"

"It wouldn't be any kind of a problem for me. And that's the truth."

"I liked your first idea better," Caroline said.

He paused for a single heartbeat. "The one about the inn?"

"Yes."

"Really?"

"Uh-huh. If you're sure you wouldn't mind."

"Mind? Of course I wouldn't mind! After what I've been going through here and what I'm bound to find piled up on my desk when I return, I'll look forward to the break!"

BRENDAN'S MEETINGS on Thursday were scheduled through to four o'clock in the afternoon. He'd warned Caroline that they might run late, and if that were the case, he'd have to take a later flight home. She had fully reconciled herself to simply seeing him on Friday after work. After all, she reasoned, that was how two good friends who just happened to be lovers would handle a brief separation. There didn't have to be any late-night reunion. They were both far too level-headed for that.

Caroline began the evening at her own place. She'd come home earlier than usual, a fact that she didn't stop to analyze, other than to tell herself she could as easily do paperwork at her kitchen table as at her office desk. That reasoning became moot, though, when the phone started to ring.

Her mother called, all in a stir about Karen's problems, but Caroline was able to fudge the facts enough to make her feel better. When, soon after that, Carl called in alarm because Madeline had suggested to him that Karen might not make it through childbirth, Caroline was able to set his brotherly heart—which she was pleased to see still functioned—to rest. She then called Karen herself and was relieved to hear her sounding a little calmer. Karen asked if she'd come to visit. Without a word about Brendan, Caroline said she'd try.

When the phone lay quiet at last, she returned to her work. She was determined to catch up on every last bit of paperwork so that if she did get to Pennsylvania for the weekend she could do so with a clear conscience.

Good intentions notwithstanding, she didn't do much catching up. She did a lot of looking at her watch and glancing across the courtyard and wondering whether Brendan had made the six-o'clock flight or had had to reschedule. When Timothy, who lived in the apartment beneath Connie, came up to borrow laundry detergent, she welcomed the momentary diversion. She did not welcome it, though, when, Ben called a few minutes later to ask if she was ready to see him. She couldn't believe the man's gall.

After calmly telling Ben what he could do with his ego, she decided that she'd had enough of the telephone for one night. Turning on the answering machine, she went to sit at the window. She felt odd, filled with a sense of anticipation that was new to her. Anticipation . . . and restlessness. She got up, wandered around the loft, returned to kneel on the window seat . . . only to repeat the circle ten minutes later.

Then inspiration struck. Slipping into a pair of sandals, she grabbed her key and Brendan's and crossed the courtyard to his building. She hadn't picked up his mail that day when she'd come home from work; it hadn't made sense, since he would be returning himself. But she did it now, brought it upstairs, then opened the windows and turned on the fan to move the air in the loft a bit.

Standing in the middle of the room, she looked around and sighed. She'd done what she'd set out to do. There was no reason why she shouldn't return to her own place.

Except that she'd be bored and restless there.

She felt better here.

It was the change of scenery, she told herself. For the past three nights she hadn't budged from her apartment. It was nice to be out. The fact that Brendan's apartment was hotter than her own didn't matter. She really did feel better here.

For several minutes she stood where she was, smiled, then sighed. She tacked loose wisps of hair into her barrette. She smiled again. She wiped the beads of sweat that dotted her nose. She sighed again. Then, nonchalantly, she scanned the apartment.

His cleaning service had been in while he'd been away, she decided, because the place was spotless. She smacked her lips together and let out a small, idle hum. So she couldn't waste a little time by cleaning.

Strolling casually toward the refrigerator, she pulled the door open and looked around. But no, she couldn't cook dinner. She had no idea what time Brendan would be arriving or whether he'd have already eaten, and anyway, *she'd* already eaten. Besides, it was hot. Not to mention that the contents of the refrigerator consisted of a carton of cottage cheese, a bottle of ketchup, a pitcher of orange juice, a half-empty box of glazed donuts that were probably stale and a sealed package of bologna. True, his freezer, like hers, was filled with frozen dinners, but she couldn't prepare him one of *those*.

She sank down on the sofa, kicked off her sandals and waited. When, no more than five minutes later, a knock came at the door, she quickly sat forward. Her heart skipped a beat or two, then settled. Brendan wouldn't knock at his own apartment.

She peered through the tiny viewer on the door, then debated for the space of several additional heartbeats. Feeling only a glimmer of unsureness, she slowly opened the door. On the other side stood the same blond-haired woman she'd previously seen only from a distance.

At the sight of Caroline rather than Brendan, Jocelyn Wills's smile got lost in a look of confusion. Her eyes flicked to the number on the door, as though she wondered whether she'd come to the wrong apartment by mistake. "Is . . , Brendan here?" she finally asked.

In that instant, Caroline could see why Brendan had felt the need to protect Jocelyn in a new city. She was lovely in a down-home, innocent, almost fragile kind of way. For that reason—and others that she didn't stop to dissect—Caroline didn't feel at all threatened by the other woman's appearance.

"You must be Jocelyn," she said with a smile that was gentle and came easily. "I'm Caroline. Brendan's told me about you."

Jocelyn dipped her head a fraction and gave a nervous smile of greeting, then sent an uneasy glance past her and repeated, almost timidly, "Is he here?"

"No. He's been out of town all week, and he's due back tonight, but I guess he must have missed his original flight if he isn't here yet."

Pressing her lips together, Jocelyn nodded. "I just wanted to say hi," she murmured, and turned to leave. "I'll catch him another time . . ."

"Uh...wait!" Caroline called out on impulse, then had the horrible notion that she was making things worse. She could clearly see that Jocelyn was disconcerted to find a woman waiting for Brendan in his apartment. She could clearly see the impression Jocelyn had gotten; Caroline was barefoot, wore a T-shirt and shorts and looked perfectly at home. She could also see that Jocelyn was going to be mortified when she got over her initial confusion.

The woman seemed so utterly alone, standing there in the hall with a questioning look on her face, that Caroline wanted to drag her inside and explain exactly what was going on between Brendan and her, and how suddenly it had come to be, and apologize for upsetting her. But that would make it worse, she realized.

She pictured Elliot with that same expression of hurt he'd worn for a fleeting instant the Friday night before. Unfortunately, to mention Elliot to Jocelyn at this moment would possibly be the most insensitive thing Caroline had ever done.

So, instead, she said with an apologetic smile, "I'll tell Brendan you came by. I'm sure he'll give you a call." Whether it had been her tone of voice, her smile or her words, something she'd done had made Jocelyn feel a little better, because she nodded a bit more confidently and then went off down the hall.

Caroline felt like a heel, but there wasn't any remedy for it. Quietly closing the door, she returned to the sofa and wondered what Brendan would think about what she'd done.

She should never have answered the door, she decided at length, but she couldn't do anything about that, either. It was done.

With a sigh, she slid lower on the leather, crossed her ankles, propped her feet on the low coffee table and let her head rest against the charcoal-brown cushion. She thought more about Jocelyn and about herself. She thought about why she felt so at home in Brendan's apartment and knew that it had little to do with the structural similarities to her own. There was something about Brendan's loft that was . . . that was . . . Brendan. She felt as comfortable here as she did in his arms. There was the same aura of safe haven, the same kind of cultured strength. And there was the same mild and subtle scent of musk and man. Of Brendan.

THERE WAS NOTHING MILD or subtle about Brendan as he took the stairs to his apartment two at a time. He'd just come from Caroline's loft, where repeated banging on the door had resulted in nothing. She couldn't be sleeping, not after his pounding, which meant that either she'd gone out or she was here. If she'd gone out, he'd be destroyed. If she was here he'd be ecstatic.

Dropping his bags so that he could fumble with his keys, he finally managed to unlock the door and shove it open. His eyes fell on the sprawled, sleeping form on his sofa and he said a quick prayer of thanks. He shifted his bags inside the apartment, quietly closed the door and, with barely a sound, crossed to where she lay.

It had been a hectic four days. He hadn't had the leisure to indulge in daydreams, but the nights, around his calls to her, had been filled with dreams. There had been times when he hadn't been able to believe that she existed. Hearing her voice had helped, but it was her skin that he wanted to feel and the warmth of her surrounding him.

He felt relief, and yes, he was ecstatic to find that she did exist and in his own apartment, no less. He also realized that he was nearly fully aroused. Looking at her did that to him. No, not just looking at her. Loving her.

He whispered those words as he bent and placed a warm kiss on her cheek. She was dead to the world, and if she did wake up and ask him what he'd said, he could play dumb and she'd think that she'd imagined the words. He whispered them again, this time with a kiss to her chin. Would she be receptive to subliminal persuasion? On the bare chance that she would, he whispered them a third time, against her neck now.

She stirred softly. Her eyes didn't open, but her arms rose to loop around his neck. She wasn't awake, exactly; she wasn't asleep, exactly. She was in that limbo between the two where pleasure could be prolonged simply by willing it so. And she did feel pleasure. Gentle kisses. Whispered words that were indistinct but infinitely reassuring. Touches and caresses that brought excitement and heat to secret spots.

She didn't have to look to know that it was Brendan who was touching her so sweetly. Her fingers told her as they wound through his hair, curved around his neck, pressed into his shoulder. Her tongue told her as it explored the inside of his mouth. Her nose told her as it inhaled the scent that had taunted her earlier but was now present in greater force, the scent that was uniquely his.

With his shirt thrust aside, she could identify him by the texture of his skin—just the right proportion of flesh to body hair to muscle and the most pleasing tone of each. She could smile at the familiarity of the small sound he made—a cross between a groan, a growl and a sigh—when she slid her hands through his open fly and touched him there in a very special way. And she could never mistake the gentleness with which he lifted her hips to free her of her shorts.

Only after he'd entered her did she open her eyes, and then it was to smile up at him for an instant before the rhythm he set caught her in its vibrant beat. With her arms coiled around his neck and her legs circling his hips, she met his fire with her own until they both succumbed to the driving heat.

That night, Caroline realized that what she had with Brendan went far beyond the simple relationship she'd envisioned at the start. It came to her in those brief, special seconds after she'd climaxed, when he was in the throes of his own powerful release and she felt the warmth he poured into her as a life force in every sense of the word. She'd never experienced as profound a sensation. She'd never known it existed—that sensation of joining with a man and, together, being part of a cosmic order.

On the one hand, it was exhilarating. On the other, it was disturbing, even frightening, because she liked what she had with Brendan. She didn't want anything to spoil it, least of all one of them taking the other too seriously. If she were, by chance, to fall in love with him, she knew that she'd be breaking the rules she herself had established.

Which might be good. Or bad. But, in any case, that possibility was going to take a lot of thought.

UNFORTUNATELY, CAROLINE didn't have much time for thought. She spent the night in Brendan's apartment, in his bed and his arms. When she returned to her own loft the next morning to shower and change for work, she found a message from her mother on the answering service.

This time the alarm was for real. While Caroline had been following passion's path to Brendan's arms, her mother had been pacing the emergency room of a hospital in Milwaukee waiting for word on her husband, who'd suffered a stroke.

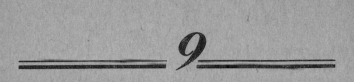

# 9

IN A RESPONSE so natural she would have thought it instinctive had it not been so new, Caroline called Brendan. She'd left no more than ten minutes before, and no more than ten minutes later he was at her loft wearing a handsome navy business suit and an expression of concern.

"I managed to reach my mother," she told him in a voice that came higher and faster than usual. "She must have been driving the nurses crazy, because they sounded relieved that I'd called. She's being her own pessimistic self, so I can't get any kind of clear picture about what's going on except that the doctors are still with him. I'm going out there."

Brendan's voice was as understanding as his eyes, and both were as supportive as the hand that held hers. "When?"

"This morning. As soon as I can get a flight."

"Have you spoken with Karen or Carl?"

She shook her head.

"Do they know?"

Again she shook her head, this time sending him a look of helplessness. "This is the last thing Karen needs to hear, given everything else that's happened to her this week. And Carl—Lord only knows how Carl will react."

"They'll have to be told."

"I know," she said on an even higher, faintly panicky note.

"Want me to call them?"

"I couldn't ask you—"

"You're not asking," he interrupted, curving warm fingers around her neck. "I'm offering. If you take your shower and pack while I make the calls, things will be a little easier, won't they?"

"Oh, yes," Caroline said, and meant it.

"Would I be better to try to catch Karen's husband and have him break the news to her?"

She considered that, then nodded quickly.

"I can easily call Carl," he went on. "How about Diane?"

"She'll want to know, too."

"Should I call her first?" Brendan asked. Behind the caution in his tone was an unspoken, even shrewd suggestion.

Caroline picked up on it with a quick nod. "Call Diane and have *her* call Carl."

It amazed Caroline that she and Brendan could be scheming to get Carl and Diane back together at a time like this. More, though, it amazed her that she was scheming with Brendan, period. Without having met a single member of her family, he seemed to know all of them well. She wondered whether she'd really talked so much about them, or whether he'd been perceptive enough to fill in the blanks, or whether he was simply that kind of caring person.

Whatever the case, she was grateful. Again there was that sense of having an ally. Actually, now, it was more having someone to lean on, to ease a bit of the weight from her shoulders. She knew that Brendan couldn't take the whole load; this was her family, her responsibility. But knowing that he was here to help with the immediate arrangements made the broader worries about her father a bit easier to handle.

Sliding her arms around him, she gave him a tight squeeze in silent expression of her gratitude. He accepted it warmly, then held her back. "Phone numbers?"

She jotted them down on a pad of paper by the phone.

"Now, shower," he urged, kissing her lightly on the forehead.

She did so and was in the midst of drying her hair when he poked his head into the bathroom. "Dan says not to worry, that he'll hold off a little bit before telling Karen so that you'll have a chance to get out to Milwaukee and hopefully call back with some news. Diane says that she'll take care of telling Carl and, by the way, thank you for calling her."

Only after Caroline had stepped into the shower had it occurred to her that letting Brendan make the calls could pose an added problem. Neither Dan nor Diane knew who he was.

"Did either of them give you any trouble?"

Brendan knew just what she meant. "I told them I was a good friend and neighbor and that I was helping you out so you could be on your way. I also called the airport, by the way. You have a flight out in an hour. That'll give you another half hour here. Enough?"

She nodded. "Enough." Setting the hair dryer down, she gave little shoves to the shoulder-length tresses, first with her brush, then with her fingers.

"Lookin' good," he said. Unable to resist taking a minute to watch her, he stood just inside the door now. Still, he'd tucked his hands in the pockets of his slacks for safekeeping. She was wrapped in a thick terry towel that was knotted just above her left breast. He envied it.

She'd already reached for her makeup and was about to apply it when she suddenly set the bottle down on the sink and turned around. Putting a hand flat on either side of his face, she stood on tiptoe and gave him a warm, wet kiss on the mouth.

"Thank you," she said, moving her fingers ever so slightly on his cheeks. "You have no idea—" Her voice cracked and broke off. Strange, her throat had grown tight, almost as though she was going to cry. But that was impossible. She never cried.

Taking a deep breath, she steadied herself and released him, then returned to her makeup.

Brendan had sensed the emotion that, for a minute, had come very close to the surface. He knew what he wanted to attribute it to, but he didn't dare. As a matter of fact, there was an awful lot that he didn't dare do, and it was beginning to bother him. With each additional minute that he spent with Caroline he grew more sure of his feelings. He tried to remind himself that barely a week had passed since they'd first gotten together, but each time he was with her he wanted her more, harder, longer, deeper, and not only physically. Hiding his feelings was becoming increasingly difficult.

But it was necessary, he reminded himself, especially now. So he thrust aside his frustrations and the dire yearning to take her in his arms, tell her that he loved her and assure her that everything would be all right, and instead asked, "Will someone cover for you at work?"

"They'd better."

"Who should I call?"

This time she shook her head. "I'll have to. I can do it while I'm packing."

He watched her for several minutes, until she'd zipped the small makeup bag. Then he asked, "Would you like anything—coffee, O.J., eggs?"

Again she shook her head. "My stomach's feeling a little off."

"What can I do? Name it and it's as good as done."

She looked up at him, her eyes large and troubled, and whispered, "Just hold me for a minute." Wrapping her arms around his neck, she closed her eyes and held tight.

It was all he could do just then not to offer to go with her. But she hadn't asked him to do it, and he didn't want to put her on the spot. It was possible that she preferred to make the trip alone. She was going to have enough to handle between her mother's mania and her father's illness, he knew, without having to worry about explaining the presence of this new man in her life.

Ironically, it was for these same reasons that he ended up on a flight to Milwaukee early Saturday morning. Caroline had called the night before to say that while her father had suffered some paralysis, he was going to be fine. Madeline Cooper was the real basket case, and the doctors' vagueness didn't help. Karen was calling regularly, and Carl was planning to fly out. Between coping with them and her mother and trying to talk with the doctors and visit her father, Caroline sounded strung out after eight short hours in Milwaukee.

So Brendan was flying out to help her. He knew that he could. He could talk with Madeline, and even if he couldn't do any better than Caroline in calming her down, at least Caroline wouldn't be taking the brunt of it.

He could also talk with the doctors. His own experience with the medical profession, obtained when his mother had had major surgery several years before, was that occasionally a deeper, louder voice was heard more quickly. He had no doubt that Caroline would have her answers in time, but if he could shorten that time, so much the better.

He could help deal with Carl when Caroline had her hands full with her mother. He could pass news on to Karen when Caroline's head ached, as she'd said it had been doing last night.

Most important, he could let Caroline lean on him when she felt pushed to the limit. It occurred to him shortly before his plane landed in Milwaukee that, at the moment, all he really wanted in life was to be there for her.

Of course, whether that was what *she* wanted was up for grabs. He knew that she'd appreciated his coming over on Friday morning. She'd told him so several times with smiles and hugs, and he'd had no cause to doubt her sincerity. But whether she'd appreciate his flying halfway across the country on her behalf was something else. He purposely hadn't told her he was coming because he hadn't wanted to give her the chance to protest.

The prospect of such a protest unsettled him as the plane landed. During the taxi ride to the hospital, he ran through the many arguments he could make to explain his presence. By the time he'd located Allan Cooper's room, he was thoroughly prepared to plead his case.

He wasn't prepared, though, for what the sight of Caroline, looking tired and pale as she sat by her father's bedside, would do to him. His insides knotted up, and he felt as though something was squeezing his heart. It was lucky that she seemed equally stunned when she looked up and saw him at the door, because it gave him a few precious minutes to recover. By the time she'd risen and come to join him, he was composed enough to launch his campaign, albeit in a low murmur appropriate to the setting.

"I don't want you to say anything about my having flown all the way out. There was nothing I really wanted to do in D.C., and I was hoping that I could be a help to you here. I'll fetch coffee, buy magazines, call nurses. I'll hold your hand." He shot a glance past her, back into the room, where the woman he assumed to be Madeline Cooper had turned and was eyeing him warily. "I'll even hold your *mother's* hand. But if I'm putting you on the spot by showing up—or if you'd really rather be alone—I'll disappear. Just say the word. Or if you want me to stay, you can explain me away as one of your partners or your secretary. You don't even have to tell your mom that I'm the same man who answered your phone when she called last weekend. We can make up a name for me. I don't care. I just wanted to be here—"

Her fingers silenced him, trembling slightly against his lips. "I have no right to want you here as much as I do," she whispered, but she didn't have time to say anything more, because at that moment Carl came flying down the hall. He held his daughter, Amy, comfortably on his hip. Diane was at his side.

Caroline hugged them all, then introduced Brendan to them as "a special someone," which seemed to satisfy them far more than the realization that they'd all been on the same plane without knowing it. Madeline, who joined them seconds later, was relieved enough to know that Carl was there with his wife and daughter to overlook the fact that Caroline's "friend" had flown all the way from Washington to be with her. By the time she thought to ask about the nature of that friendship, Brendan was proving to be such a source of strength that she didn't bother to question and simply accepted what seemed perfectly right and natural.

He was, in his unobtrusive way, like another member of the family. Madeline turned to him as nearly as often as she turned to Caroline, which didn't bother him in the least. He was in a far better frame of mind to take Madeline's alarmism than Caroline, who was busy trying to find out how alarmed she should rightly be.

As it happened, Allan Cooper's stroke proved to be less severe than it had seemed at the start. He had a slight paralysis on his left side that the doctors believed would respond well to therapy, and he was awake, aware and easily able to make himself understood by the time Caroline and Brendan bade him goodbye on Sunday afternoon.

Caroline was surprised that she was able to leave so easily. She'd assumed that she'd have felt obliged to stay and hold her mother's hand a bit longer. But everything was under control. She was convinced that her dad was receiving the best of care and that Madeline would be a nervous Nellie regardless. Besides, Carl had decided to stay on an extra few days with Diane and Amy. Amy had proven to be the only one capable of distracting Madeline for long, which was working out conveniently. Carl and Diane had begun to talk and smile with each other as they hadn't done in months and months, and they could use whatever time they found to be alone together.

But Caroline's thoughts weren't on her parents, Amy, Carl or Diane as the plane took off and headed east. Her thoughts were on Brendan. His presence had taken the weekend from the ranks of an ordeal and transformed it into something a little less daunting. She felt calm, and that was a definite improvement over the way her family usually made her feel.

Brendan was a diffuser. He'd taken the sharp tip off the crisis and softened its edges. He was her friend and confidante. He shared the burden of responsibility and helped her put things into perspective. And he was a steady reminder that she was more than just Caroline-the-last-hope-of-the-needy. There had been times that weekend when they were alone, when he would hold her hand or wrap an arm around her shoulder or draw her head to his chest, and she would feel valued and appreciated as a person in her own right, totally aside from any service she had to offer. And when, very late on Saturday night when the rest of the household was asleep, he made hot, sweet, silent love to her, she felt positively cherished.

Brendan was wonderful, but that was precisely what began to bother her during that flight home on Sunday. He fit so easily into her life that thought of life without him was suddenly frightening. In little over a week, she had grown dependent on him. It wasn't a material dependence; she felt every bit as self-sufficient as she ever had in the sense of day-to-day, surface functioning. But emotionally...she'd quickly come to need him that way.

Theoretically, she reasoned, everything should be perfect. She'd met a man who interested and excited her, a man who was strong enough to stand on his own two feet and take some of her weight, as well. They could head off into the sunset and live happily ever after, knowing that between them they had a handle on the world.

But it wasn't as simple as that. For one thing, a mere nine days ago she'd announced—no, insisted—that their relationship should be fun and free. If, by her own decree, she'd ruled out thoughts of a future, could she simply reverse herself now and expect that Brendan would go along?

For another thing, life often got complicated when couples started thinking in terms of long-range commitments. General concerns became personal. Issues that had previously been overlooked suddenly came to the fore. Expectations changed and sides were taken. She knew that from her work. Time and again she'd counseled couples who couldn't understand why their relationship had been perfect until they'd gotten married.

She asked herself if her work had turned her off marriage and knew that the answer was no. She'd seen many long-lasting, happy marriages—her parents' included—but she knew, too, of the growing pains those relationships occasionally suffered. She didn't want *any* pains in her relationship with Brendan.

She asked herself if her experience with Ben was making her nervous, and again the answer was no. Ben was an egocentric man who had a way with words that had little to do with honest, gut-wrenching emotion. Ben was as different from Brendan as night from day, and just as there was no comparison between the men, there was no comparison between the relationship she had with each.

The trouble was that she couldn't define exactly what she wanted her relationship with Brendan to be. Was it to be laid-back and hassle free, or more intense? Could it be both? Could it *not* be both?

The plane landed in Washington without a hitch, but Caroline was still grappling with the dilemma that night as she lay in bed with Brendan. Tipping her head sideways on the pillow, she studied him in the dark. He had a strong profile—all the way from the dark spikes of hair falling over his brow to the blunt tips of his well-formed toes.

They'd just made love. His skin gleamed beneath a sheen of sweat that hadn't yet dried in the hot night air. His body hair was ruffled, left that way by the impassioned movements of her skin on his. His muscles were relaxed, his breathing steady. He'd fallen asleep.

She couldn't begrudge him that. He'd been a rock for her this weekend. He'd earned his rest. And besides, she didn't want to talk right now. She wasn't ready to share the particular thoughts in her mind.

So she wrestled with them silently for another hour, until sheer exhaustion wore her down. But before she fell asleep, she reached a decision. Brendan Carr was too good to be believed. He had to have a flaw. It was going to be up to her to find that flaw, before she was so head over heels in love with the man that she was beyond redemption.

DURING THE NEXT FEW WEEKS, Caroline and Brendan settled into a routine that wasn't so much a routine as a regular meeting of minds. They each went to work in the morning and brought work home to do at night, but there was variety in where they did that work—sometimes at his loft, sometimes at hers. There was variety, too, in when they did it—sometimes before they went to a late movie, sometimes after they returned from a restaurant, sometimes between snacks or phone calls or chores. They found the spontaneous little twists to be refreshing, and though they discovered small differences in their tastes, compromise was incredibly simple.

Caroline wasn't quite as gung-ho about looking for Brendan's flaws as she should have been. Too often she was so comfortable with him that she simply didn't think to look for flaws, and when she was tired after a day of work, she didn't want to look for them.

On occasion, though, when an odd, tiny inner unease nudged her, she would examine their lives together and search for a catch in the relationship. She'd wanted the freedom to come and go as she liked, and she had it. Brendan never made her feel guilty. He didn't say things he didn't mean or make promises he didn't keep. She was able to lean on him and find ready support, and not once had he treated her like his mother. When she looked for signs that she was being taken advantage of, she couldn't find a one.

Cooking dinner was a case in point. On those nights when they decided to eat in, she took charge, since it had quickly become clear that even she knew more about cooking than he did. But he helped. Even when she protested, he offered, insisting on chopping onions or tenderizing steaks or setting the table, and not once was she left to do the cleanup alone.

Doing laundry was another example. Without a second thought, Caroline offered to throw his laundry in with hers when she went to the basement washing machine. It was no sweat off her back, she'd reasoned; she was doing the wash anyway, and the addition of his T-shirts, shorts and socks was negligible. In turn, Brendan insisted on making the trip to the dry cleaner's that she would have also had to make. The following week, when she'd gotten her period and was feeling crampy and under the weather, he did both chores without pause.

No, she wasn't being taken advantage of. True, she automatically straightened things up when she was at his loft. But then, he automatically answered the phone when he was at hers. True, she took care of his newspapers and mail when he was out of town. But then, he called every night from wherever he was, and when he came home he was more solicitous than ever, compensating for what she'd done while he was gone.

It was while he was on one such trip, after they'd been together for nearly four weeks, that a knock came at Brendan's door. Having left work immediately after her last appointment, Caroline had been waiting for just that knock. She said a tiny prayer that was answered the instant she opened the door and saw the pretty brunette who was no more than sixteen and very, very nervous.

"You're Shelley," she announced softly but with an excited smile. Catching the girl's hand, she drew her into the loft and quickly shut the door. "I'm Caroline. Thank goodness you've come. Your mother's been worried."

Shelley seemed a little perturbed by that. "She shouldn't have worried. I left a note saying I was coming here."

"Still, Kansas City to Washington's a long way. How did you do it?"

"Bus."

Caroline hated to think of the state of the nation's bus stops, but at least the girl hadn't hitchhiked. "Your brother will be relieved to see you."

Shelley glanced uneasily around the loft. "Is he here?"

"He's been out of town since yesterday morning, but when he learned that you were on your way, he canceled his meetings for tomorrow. He should be back here in an hour or two."

Shelley nodded. Her gaze skittered off. She was using her forefinger to pick at her thumb. She looked awkward. "Were you the one who talked with my mom?"

"Uh-huh."

"Are you living here with Brendan?"

"No."

"But you must have something going with him if you were here."

Caroline hadn't been sure how Shelley would react to her. She was relieved to find that the girl was more curious than hostile. "I had dropped some things off last night and happened to be here when your mother called."

"I'll bet Mom was surprised when you answered the phone instead of Brendan."

"A little, I think." Caroline's smile was crooked as she recalled how impressed she'd been with the older woman's aplomb. "She recovered."

"She always does. She's cool. I have to say that for her."

The awkwardness seemed to be easing. Caroline took advantage of that and suggested softly, "Think we ought to give her a call and tell her you arrived safely?"

"She'll probably be furious with me once she knows I'm safe."

"Because you left a note and took off, rather than discussing the trip with her beforehand? Maybe. But if you call right now and tell her that you just this minute arrived and wanted to call right away because you knew she'd be worried, I bet the anger will be minimal."

Apparently that made some sense to Shelley, because after a brief pause, she let her backpack slide to the floor and went to the phone.

In an effort to give her a little privacy, Caroline crossed to the French windows and stood with her back to the girl. She could easily begin to understand why Brendan held a soft spot in his heart for this half sister who was so much younger than he. She was adorable to look at—slim and petite, dressed in ankle socks and flats, a short denim skirt that was nearly hidden first by a large Banana Republic T-shirt, then by an even larger denim work shirt with sleeves rolled high and lapels flapped open. Caroline's trained eye saw a sweetness and a certain vulnerability in her, which fit well into what Brendan's mother had told her the night before.

Shelley wasn't rebellious. The girl's father—Brendan's mother's second husband—had died three years before, and Shelley and her mother were close. Shelley didn't drink or do drugs. She was a top student in school and, a late developer, had just become part of a social group during the past year. Her one fault, it seemed, was laziness, which was why she didn't have a job for the summer. She'd been spending her time between her girlfriends and her first steady boyfriend. Two nights ago, she and the boy had broken up, which was why she'd taken off in search of Brendan, whom she adored.

"Caroline?"

Caroline whipped around at the sound of her name to see Shelley holding out the phone. She quickly retrieved it. "Hello?"

"Well, she sounds all right," Elizabeth Plummer said without preamble.

"And she looks fine."

"She says that she'd like to stay with Brendan for a few days. I know that his place is small, so it may be a problem, but he'll have to be the one to decide. Would you have him call me when he gets home?"

"Sure thing."

"And you won't let Shelley budge from there until he does?"

"She's not going anywhere," Caroline said with a mischievous grin for Shelley. "I'm lonely. I need company." She shifted the phone away from her mouth to ask Shelley if she'd had dinner. When the girl shook her head, Caroline said into the phone, "We're both starved. Brendan has a London broil in the fridge that I think I'll do on the hibachi. If he times it right, he may walk in just in time for the feast."

"Thank you, Caroline," his mother said with sincerity. "Perhaps one day I'll be able to thank you in person."

"I'd like that," Caroline said with a gentle smile, then added a goodbye and hung up the phone.

Brendan did, indeed, time things right. He walked into the loft with just enough time to spare to give bear hugs to both Caroline and Shelley before sitting down to a feast of London broil, garlic bread and salad—all of which Caroline had picked up on her way home from work.

Shelley camped out on Brendan's sofa for five days, during which time Caroline stayed at her own loft. Though Caroline missed Brendan's loving and the feel of his long body beside her at night, the arrangements were for the best. Caroline's close relationship with Brendan was obvious enough to Shelley, who craved a little of her brother's attention. Granting Shelley that time alone with him minimized the possibility of jealousy.

Caroline and Shelley became friends. Ironically, while Shelley had thought Brendan would be the one to whom she would pour out her broken heart, she found that Caroline, being that much closer to her age and a woman, was even better for the role. Caroline had two other advantages: she was one step removed from family, and she knew what she was doing.

By the time Shelley left to return home—by plane this time—she had decided that her heart wasn't quite as badly broken as she'd originally thought. She had also decided that Caroline would make a perfect wife for Brendan, and she proceeded to tell it to her mother, who called and told it to Brendan himself, who said that he agreed with her and that he was working on it.

He was working on it. He was working on it. He'd told himself that so many times that he was sick of the words. Unfortunately, "working on it" most often meant sitting back and doing nothing but being himself in the hope that he could get far enough under Caroline's skin to force some kind of eruption of feeling. For a man who was used to action, the wait was tedious. But he had no choice.

Circumstance was on his side. The circumstance of Caroline's father's stroke had brought them to Milwaukee, where Brendan had been able to show Caroline not only that he could get along with her family but that life with them was easier for her when he was around. The circumstance of Shelley Plummer's broken heart had brought Caroline into contact with Brendan's family, with positive feelings all around.

But the circumstance of the birth of Karen's baby was the most emotionally enlightening for Caroline. The baby arrived, quite conveniently, on a Friday, three days after Shelley left. Caroline got the call from Dan at work and was beside herself with glee. She spent her lunch hour shopping for her new nephew, then insisted on dragging Brendan out that evening to pick up even more. Because he was so delighted that she was so delighted, he went without a peep.

The next morning, they drove to Philadelphia. Karen was ebullient. She'd found labor to be easier than pregnancy, and she and Dan were overjoyed with their son. They took well to Brendan, too, and the feelings were mutual. That helped Caroline, because with Brendan preoccupied with Karen and Dan, she had more time to spend on the phone reassuring her mother that the baby was healthy. When she wasn't doing that, she stood at the nursery window staring down at the small, snugly swathed bundle of life that was the product of the love between Karen and Dan.

Thin, purple eyelids shifting with each newborn dream. A tiny mouth that formed sweet shapes around nothing at all. Miniature fingers, like spider's legs, crawling idly across a pink cheek. A nose that was little more than a bump with two holes at the bottom.

He was precious, Caroline thought, and he touched her deeply. She recalled the time when her niece had been born four years before. She'd been excited then and a little frightened.

Now she was touched in a different way. It was no great mystery. She was a woman, with maternal instincts, and those instincts were making themselves known. She wanted to hold, to nurture and to love a baby that was every bit as small and helpless as this one. She wanted a baby of her own—one that was hers and Brendan's.

Caroline thought about that through what was left of the afternoon. She and Brendan took Dan out to dinner. Then, dropping him back at the hospital to be with his wife and son, they drove north into the country to the inn they'd picked from Caroline's book.

Brendan, too, was pensive. He was thinking many of the same things Caroline was, and he knew it. He'd seen her face—how could he have *helped* but see her face—when she'd been looking at that infant. He'd never seen such an exquisite expression, and while he marveled at the beauty behind it, he was annoyed that it wasn't *his* baby that she was looking at with such awe. She would make a magnificent mother; he'd known it even before he'd met her face-to-face, and his judgment hadn't changed. But, damn it, before they had kids they had to get married, and before they got married they had to declare that they were in love, and before they did that, Caroline had to realize that the relationship she'd *thought* she wanted wasn't enough!

Words and emotions swirled within him. Having no outlet, they coiled around themselves. By the time he and Caroline had reached their destination, a charming inn in Quakertown, he'd worked himself into a mood that was as lousy as it was uncharacteristic.

"I'm going for a run," he told her as soon as they'd been shown to their room. He busied himself digging a pair of running shorts out of his bag.

Caroline had been aware of his mood from that moment when it had crossed the line from disturbed to angry. It was almost as though she'd felt invisible fingers tapping on her shoulder, telling her that something was brewing. But to know something was brewing was one thing; to act on that knowledge was something else. She had a vague idea what was on his mind. She just wasn't sure she was ready to discuss it.

"It's dark out," she said.

"I often run at night."

"These roads aren't lit like the ones at home."

He'd pushed down his jeans and was sitting on the edge of the bed trying to work them over his sneakers. When the denim didn't budge, he gave an impatient growl. "There's a moon," he said as he tugged off the sneakers, then the jeans, then pulled on the running shorts and went at relacing the sneakers.

Caroline hadn't ever seen him quite this way. She'd seen him when he'd been frustrated by something at work and had come home scowling. She'd seen him when he'd gone out one morning to find that the tires of his car had been slashed. She'd even seen him when Shelley had told him where she'd spent the night between Kansas City and Washington.

But he'd never scowled at *her* before—not that he was doing so now. He wasn't looking at her at all. And that was almost worse!

At a loss, she watched him finish with the sneakers, whip his shirt over his head and toss it aside, then leave the room. Turning out the light, she went to the window in time to see his shadowed form leave the shelter of the inn and take off at a rhythmic run down the drive.

She stood there long after he'd disappeared from sight, finally settling into a plush wing chair to await his return. After a while, it occurred to her that she was envious. He wasn't the only one in need of a little fresh air. Changing into her own shorts and sneakers, she nodded her way past the few guests who were sitting in the lobby and left the inn.

Once outside, she was faced with the dilemma of what to do and where to go. She wasn't a runner, and even if she were, she couldn't have known what direction Brendan had taken when he'd hit the main road.

She didn't want to miss him. Forget the business about getting fresh air; what she'd really come out for was to be with Brendan.

# 10

CAROLINE SAT against the tall white pillar that was rooted to the front steps of the inn. Her hands were clasped between her knees, while her eyes systematically swept the darkened landscape for signs of life. She wondered where Brendan had gone and when he'd be back, but more, she wondered what he'd been thinking about when he'd taken off that way.

Nervously, she jumped up from the step and wandered into the yard, but the restless pacing she did there accomplished nothing. Minutes dragged by, and he didn't return.

The night was hot. Her skin was damp and sticky. She swatted at a bug, idly at first, then with greater determination when the bug persisted in hovering by her ear.

In a spurt of impatience, she marched down the broad walk to the drive, where she stood for several minutes, searching the night. Brendan had been gone, by her guess, for nearly an hour. She couldn't imagine that he'd been running the whole time. The air was nearly as humid as it had been in Washington, not ideal for a prolonged jog. Taking a page from her mother's book, she envisioned him passing out by the roadside and lying there unattended or, worse, being hit by a car. She went on to consider the possibility that he'd been accosted; violence was known to rise in the heat of the summer, and indeed, the moon was full.

All of which speculation was absurd, she scoffed silently. The man earned his livelihood tracking down terrorists. *That* was dangerous. There was no danger on a quiet country road on a peaceful night beneath the stars. Most likely he was in town drinking a nice, cool beer.

Retracing her steps to the front porch, she sat down again. Something was wrong. Somewhere, somehow, she and Brendan had stopped communicating. That had been one of the basic rules she'd set—that there be honesty and openness between them. But right now there wasn't. She had the distinct feeling that Brendan was angry, and she wasn't quite sure why.

Once again she left the front steps, this time to wander down the drive and, in sheer frustration, start along the street. She didn't have to go far. No more than a three-minute walk from the inn was a low stone wall. Straddling that wall was her man.

She felt relief, then trepidation, but there was no way she could have turned around and left him alone. So she approached slowly. Moonlight glistened on his sweaty skin, and his hair was tousled. His breathing was regular, though; she guessed that he'd been sitting there for a time.

"Did you run?" she asked lightly.

He shrugged. "A little."

"Too hot?"

"Yeah."

Three feet of thick night air separated them. While Caroline found the air to be oppressive, the separation was worse. This was Brendan . . . her dream lover . . . the man to whom she could say anything and everything . . . the friend with whom she could carry on the most exciting of silent talks.

But neither of them was talking now, and there was nothing comfortable about the silence. She wanted to cry. Instead, she asked, "Are you hungry?"

"No."

"I'll bet you could use a cool drink."

He didn't respond to that at all but looked down, breaking eye contact for the first time since she'd come along.

Caroline moved closer. "What's wrong, Brendan?"

It was a long time before he answered. He plucked at stray blades of grass that grew in spikes between the rocks, tossing each aside after he'd mangled it. She was beginning to wonder whether he planned to answer at all when his arms fell limply to his sides and he raised his eyes to the branches overhead. His voice came slowly and sounded distant.

"That was incredible today... seeing that little baby. I haven't ever seen a human being that small."

Caroline was surprised. She hadn't expected that he'd still be thinking of the baby. She watched him closely as he frowned, then lowered his head and, still frowning, concentrated on the stone wall between his thighs.

"It struck me..." he said, then hesitated. "Well, lots of things struck me, but the first thing was that that little boy is totally helpless. Without his parents or a nurse or some kind of caretaker, he dies. That's it. He just dies. Totally helpless. Totally dependent on others for survival."

He stopped talking. He brushed his thumb back and forth over the rock. His lower lip came out to cover its mate, sliding free at length. "And then I started thinking of survival, and it hit me that we really take having kids for granted. We don't think of it as propagating the species, but that's what it is. There's something primal about it, something raw . . . basic."

He paused for a brief, pensive minute. "We're like animals in that way, and I don't mean it in a negative sense. People regard 'animal behavior' as synonymous with lust, but the fact is that animals do what they have to, to keep their species from becoming extinct. The knowledge is built-in. Instinct tells them what to do and when to do it." He gave a soft snort. "It's ironic. We have the superior ability to reason, and because of that our timing gets screwed up. Not that there's a risk of our becoming extinct. . . ."

His voice trailed off. He remained still for a bit, only his thumbs moving on the rock. Then, slowly and uncertainly, he lifted his gaze to Caroline's. "I was terrified when I saw that baby. I was terrified thinking of the responsibility involved—not only to feed it and clothe it but to love it and educate it and raise it to be a productive individual." He took a breath, stopped, then asked, "Do you ever think of things like that?"

She nodded.

"I'll bet they don't frighten you."

"Sure they do," she answered softly. "Raising a child is a challenge no matter how you look at it. There are some things that start me shaking."

"Like what?"

"Like what happens if the baby's sick and crying and I don't know what to do and I can't reach a doctor."

"That's an emergency situation. Any normal parent would be scared."

"Some of the everyday, nonemergency things scare me, too. Like holding the baby when it's small and fragile and squirming. And protecting the soft spot at the top of its head. And making sure that it doesn't fall out of the crib or off the dressing table or down a flight of stairs." She took a breath. "The responsibility is awesome."

Brendan was studying her intently. His voice came out deeper, a little husky. "But then, in spite of those fears, you look at a baby like we were looking at Karen's today, and you know that you want one. That you have to have one. And you start thinking that if you should be struck by lightning and killed tomorrow or next week or next year—"

"Shh!" She cut him off with a sharp sound and a hand on his shoulder. Her hand remained tight on his flesh, though her tone softened. "Don't say that."

"But there's always the possibility. Life isn't forever."

"You're only thirty-eight years old!"

"Which is damned close to middle age—if I'm lucky. Hell, I don't know what the future holds—"

"Brendan!" she protested, but he went quickly on.

"It suddenly occurred to me that if I don't have a child, I really don't have anything to leave behind. A son or daughter is a person's legacy to the world. It's a little bit of him that lives on to be passed to another generation, and another. If I want to have that child and imprint it with *me*, I'd better get going."

Caroline had swung a leg over the stone wall and come down close behind him. "It's not like you to be so morbid."

"Not morbid. Realistic."

"Morbid," she insisted, sliding her arms around his waist. She proceeded to punctuate each word with a squeeze. "Nothing's going to happen to you. You'll have those children, and they'll do you proud."

He half turned his head toward his shoulder and vowed, "That's what I want, Caroline. I want to have kids, and maybe it's arrogant of me to say this, but they'll be great. They'll be bright and personable and enterprising." He dropped his gaze to the spot at his waist where her fingers were threaded and raised a hand to touch them. "When I was looking at that baby today, I could almost see my own. I could almost feel it, feel the way it would feel in my arms, the touch of its skin. That has never, never happened to me—" His voice broke and he fell silent.

"Oh, Brendan," Caroline whispered. Her eyes were closed and she was moving her cheek on his skin. She'd felt it, too—that elemental urge when she'd been looking at Karen's baby—and she felt the same elemental urge now. It was an ache deep in her womb, and there was nothing objective or detached about it. It was intricately connected to this man. She'd never been one to believe in predestination, but there was something so inevitable about her attraction for him that she couldn't have fought it if she'd wanted to. But she didn't want to fight it. She could still be honest in this. She'd always been honest in her physical need for him.

Her fingers spread over the warm, flat muscles of his stomach. She identified one rib, then another, and as her hands rose so did her excitement. Her name came as a quiet whisper on his lips, goading her on. She pressed closer to his back until her breasts were flattened. Her palms made slow, repeated crossings over his hardening nipples.

Brendan had never pretended to be immune to her touch, and he didn't now. But the pleasure was deeper, the need greater. Something of frightening force simmered just beneath the surface. In an attempt to keep it restrained, he inhaled sharply and pressed his palms flat to his thighs. But he couldn't keep his head from falling back in pleasure, or his back from arching, or his chest from swelling to her touch.

So many times in the past month they'd made love, yet for Caroline touching Brendan now took on new purpose. His responses were quick—the tightening of his muscles, the increasing speed of his pulse and shallowness of his breathing. They were prescribed responses, the wordless preamble to lovemaking. They were responses relevant to the biological drive not only to mate but to mate well.

Caroline understood the power of that drive. She'd already accepted the fact that if she were to have a baby, she'd want Brendan to father it. That knowledge, combined with the incredible inundation of sensation that came with the feel of his skin beneath her mouth; his taste; his scent, turned her on.

Her hands grew more active, venturing farther and more boldly. She wasn't thinking of teasing him or even of pleasuring him. She was simply arousing him to a state where he could fulfill his function as a man. And he was fast getting there. When she lowered her hands to his nylon running shorts, she felt the strained gloving of his sex. She caressed him there; he made a low, almost primitive sound. Needing to touch his flesh, she breached the band of his shorts and cupped him with both hands. He made another sound, one that she echoed. Touching him was setting her afire.

She wanted him desperately, but words would have shattered the precious silence of the night. So she showed him her need by making slow, undulating movements against him while her fingers drew him to his limits with silken strokes.

In a swing so gentle that it might have been made in slow motion, Brendan turned and brought her down to the grass on the hidden, meadow side of the wall. There was nothing slow about his fever, though. His mouth was open and hot on hers. His body was insistent. His large hands freed her of her shorts in the same deft movements with which he stripped himself. Claiming his place between her waiting thighs, he entered her with the sureness of divine plan.

Their lovemaking, then, became something fierce and urgent. The pace was fast. Gentleness was something that neither of them could afford. Brendan's thrusts were deep and vibrant; Caroline met each with greater demand, then cried out when he gave her what she craved. She'd wrapped her legs high around his waist, inviting the deepest possible penetration, and he was there, touching the mouth of her womb, over and over again.

The night woods were a mute witness to the futile battle they waged. Their bodies grew wet with sweat and taut with need, and when the strain of passion erupted into a pulsing climax, they cried out.

But they'd failed. There would be no baby, because they were sane, responsible individuals who left nothing to chance when it came to conception.

Caroline was protected. A strange word, protected. In the aftermath of this night's passion, it was something to be resented. And a short while later, as Caroline and Brendan walked side by side back to the inn, they shared a sadness that compounded itself by their inability to discuss it.

THEY SPENT THE NIGHT making fast, furious, demanding love. It seemed the only way they could express their feelings. There was a desperation to their coming together, an element of punishment in the fury of their coupling. And between bouts of passion, there was sadness.

By noon the next day they were back at the hospital in Philadelphia, and by five that afternoon, in Washington. They'd talked little during the trip. The silence was a knife twisting in Caroline, but she simply couldn't break it. There was so much to say that she couldn't say a thing, and what she had to say was of such import that she didn't know how to begin.

Brendan didn't have that problem. At her open door, he took her hand, whispered a soft kiss to its palm, then released it. "Go on in," he said softly.

"You're not coming?"

"No."

"Maybe later?"

"I don't think so."

The pain in his eyes became her own as understanding dawned. "It's not because you're tired or because you have work to do."

He shook his head.

"You want out," she said, trying to still the suddenly torturous pounding of her heart.

"No. But I can't go on this way. I need something more."

"I can't give you what you want?"

"You can, but I'm not sure you will. I want it all, Caroline. I want the commitment, the strings, the ties, the hassles. That bargain we made—it just doesn't work for me anymore."

The pounding in her chest had congealed into a painfully tight band that made breathing difficult. Her throat ached. Her eyes filled with tears. She pressed her lips together when they seemed prone to tremble and spoke only when she felt she had a modicum of control. "You want marriage."

"Yes. Marriage, kids, the works, and I want them with you. But you have to decide if that's what you want." His hand came up to trace the delicate line of her jaw, and he seemed a little awed for a minute. By the time he returned his gaze to hers, though, the pain was back. "I realize that I'm older than you are. I've been around longer, so I know what I want when I see it. You may not be as sure. That's why I think we should cool it."

She swallowed, trying to maintain a certain poise. "I don't understand. If you want to be with me for the rest of your life, why should we cool it?"

"Because when we're together, we don't think critically, and right now you have to think critically. You have to decide one way or another, Caroline. I can't wait." He thrust a hand through his hair. "I just can't wait. I told myself that I could. I told myself that if I was patient you'd reach the same conclusions I had. But you haven't, and there are times when I hurt so much inside from wanting you that I think I'll go mad." A little short on composure, he took in an uneven breath. "I want to say those words, Caroline. I know you don't want to hear them, because Ben misused them and one of the things you didn't want in our relationship was bartering with vows and promises. At some point, though, you have to trust me enough to know that when I say them I mean them." His voice grew pleading. "Can't you *feel* what I feel?"

She continued to look up at him through brimming tears. But she couldn't speak. She was afraid.

Brendan put the last of his cards on the table. "If I asked you to marry me right now, would you say yes?"

Marriage was the ultimate tie and could be the ultimate hassle if things didn't work out. She wished he hadn't done it this way. She needed a slower approach. She needed time to think. "We've only known each other . . . it's only been . . ."

"See? You're not sure. We could go on forever as we are now, and maybe you'd be happy, but not me. So what I'm suggesting may not make sense, but I don't know what else to do."

Caroline bit hard on her lower lip. She felt her nose running from the strain of holding in tears, and even then Brendan's face blurred. "Maybe you're right," she whispered as she lowered her eyes.

It wasn't what Brendan wanted to hear. He'd been half-hoping his suggestion alone would have been enough to force an admission of love from her. The fact that it hadn't done so left open the possibility that she didn't love him as much as he'd thought. She was obviously upset now, but he had no way of knowing if that was simply because she was losing a friend. His agony increased, but there was no turning back.

"Let me know when you've made up your mind," he said. Fearing for his poise, he leaned forward, kissed her lightly, even lingeringly, on the forehead, then turned and left.

CAROLINE SUFFERED through Sunday night with an awful ache inside. She felt a deathly loss, and as many times as she prayed for numbness, it never came.

Going to work on Monday was a help. Her clients demanded the kind of concentration that offered a relief from her private thoughts, but no sooner had each client left than she felt the burden return like chain mail settling over her heart.

On Monday night she talked with her mother, who was in a snit about the bossiness of her father's physical therapist, and with Diane, who called to ask about Karen's baby. In the process of the latter, the discussion turned to Carl and issues of communication. Caroline was beginning to feel like a fraud by the time she hung up the phone.

On Tuesday, Elliot stopped in at her office to see her. He was meeting his brother for lunch, he said, and had just wanted to say hello. She sensed that he was testing the waters, but, if so, he was in for a disappointment. She was polite, but her mind was elsewhere. He'd have had to be blind not to see it and deaf not to hear it.

By Wednesday morning, Caroline felt as though she'd been rolled through a wringer. She hadn't slept well in four days. She wasn't in the mood to see individual clients, much less the group she had scheduled. So it was probably just as well that the sheriff chose that time to serve her. She took a good long look at the papers he presented, sank back in her chair in confusion, then rose in anger and, pausing only long enough to let Maren know she was leaving, took off.

She'd never seen Brendan at work, but everyone knew where the Justice Department was, and once there, she had no trouble finding his office. He was with another man. They both looked up when she appeared at the door. Brendan's eyes widened and his color faded a little. He turned to the man with him and asked in a voice of quiet command that belied the question, "Can we pick up on this later?"

The man closed his folder, nodded to Caroline and left. The instant the door shut, she advanced on the desk and slapped down the papers she'd been all but crushing in her hand.

Brendan had been too busy taking in her appearance to notice the papers. Her outfit, a soft, flowing skirt and a short-sleeved, lightweight cotton sweater, was appropriate for her work. But the strand of pearls around her neck was crooked, her hair was disheveled and high color stained her cheeks. She looked spectacular, vibrant and alive. She also looked furious.

He dropped his gaze to the papers. "What're these?"

She was standing straight, fists clenched at her sides. Her voice had that higher-than-normal pitch that it always got when she was upset. "I was hoping you could tell me. They were delivered to my office a little while ago."

Brendan read the papers, then looked up at Caroline in confusion. "Who is Paul Valente?"

"He's that client I told you about, the one whose wife walked out on our sessions. He's been seeing me alone since then—remember, I told you?—and now *she's* naming me in an alienation-of-affection suit! Have you ever heard anything so stupid?"

Brendan had heard plenty of things even more stupid when it came to the law and would have told her so, but before he'd had a chance, she was racing on.

"Nothing like this has ever happened to me before! It's insulting—to think that I'd actively pit a husband and wife against each other. I'm a *professional*. A professional doesn't do things like that!"

Brendan held out a hand to calm her, but she thought he was arguing, so she said, "I know what you're going to say—that the papers are full of stories of psychiatrists taking sexual advantage of their patients—but that isn't applicable here. I've only seen the man four times, and each time it was in the middle of the afternoon, with my partners in adjoining offices. Other than those four times, I saw Paul and Sheila together. I thought I had a reasonable working relationship with them both. How could she turn on me this way?"

Brendan was thinking of the adage about a woman scorned, which would explain some of Sheila Valente's fury, but he remembered Caroline saying that Sheila walked out on Paul, rather than vice versa, so the adage didn't apply. "She's probably—"

"There's no 'probably' about it," Caroline cried. "She's *crazy*, and the thing that bothers me most is that through all those months of therapy I didn't see it. I regarded her as an egotistical but basically rational woman. Now look what she's done!" She pointed a shaking finger at the accusatory papers. "Correct me if I'm wrong, but when someone is charged with 'alienation of affection,' they're being charged with more than talk. That witch is accusing me of chasing after her husband. The implication is that I *slept* with him, which is the dumbest thing I've heard yet!"

"Caroline—" Brendan began. He sensed that she was on the edge of hysteria, which wasn't like her at all. She might be a sight for his starving eyes, but that didn't mean that he couldn't see how tense she was.

"Do you know what this could do? This could ruin my career!"

"It won't—"

"If word gets out that I'm seducing my clients, I could be finished. I don't think I could bear that, Brendan," she said. Tears were quickly gathering in her eyes. "Because I'm not guilty of a thing. I tried my best with Paul and Sheila, and when Sheila gave up, I tried my best with Paul alone. Isn't that what you said—that what really mattered was whether you've tried your best?"

He was up and rounding the desk. She'd begun to tremble, and he needed to touch her. He'd gotten as far as clasping her arms when her composure started to crumble.

"I mean, the charge is absurd," she said brokenly. She was looking up at him, pleading, and the first of her tears had begun to trickle slowly down her cheeks. "The idea that I c-could have been with someone else...that I could have tried to seduce Paul or even wanted to do it...when a-all along I couldn't possibly think about any other man because I've been in love with you . . ."

With that, she lost it completely. She closed her eyes and tucked her head low. Her hands came up to cover her face and muffle the sobs she couldn't control. In the next minute, those sobs were muffled against Brendan's shirtfront as he wrapped her tightly in his arms.

"Shh," he whispered into her hair. "It's okay, baby, it's okay."

Incredibly, she began to cry even harder. Her arms slid around his neck, and she clung to him as though someone would be taking him away any minute. "Bren . . . dan . . ."

He held her tighter and murmured soft, soothing sounds. Her tears hurt him, but he knew that she needed the outlet. He'd seen how closely she'd guarded her tears on Sunday night, and he guessed that she hadn't let herself cry even after he'd left. He wondered when she'd last cried, really cried as she was doing now.

"Brendan . . . oh . . ."

"I love you, sweetheart."

"I've been . . . so . . . stupid. . . ."

"No, you haven't."

She burst into a new round of sobs, and he could do nothing but hold her tightly until she'd calmed a bit. At that point, he backed up to sit on the edge of the desk. Digging into the small purse that hung from her shoulder, he fished out a Kleenex. Then he shifted her sideways against his chest, handed her the Kleenex and watched while she blotted her eyes. He used the tips of his fingers to smooth her hair back from her face.

"Don't worry about the lawsuit," he said softly.

She sniffled.

"I guarantee you the charges will be dropped long before anything comes of it."

"Mmm."

"It's not uncommon for a husband or wife to go a little bit off the deep end in the course of a divorce. We'll explain the facts to Sheila Valente's lawyer, and if she persists in going forward, we'll threaten to countersue. She'll change her mind."

"I know."

"You do?"

Caroline nodded. Her head was still bowed, and the Kleenex was a tight wad in the fist that was pressed to his chest. "I just needed to see you." She took a breath that was so uneven he thought she was going to start crying again. She didn't. Nor did she look up. "It's been an awful week without you. Getting those papers was just one more lousy thing, but if it hadn't been that, it would have been something else. I've felt stifled not being able to talk with you. I've looked across the courtyard—"

"Only after you turned out the lights," he interrupted. "Before that, you never looked once. I was watching."

"After I turned out the lights," she admitted softly.

"Why not before?"

She thought about that for a minute. "Because—" she took a breath "—because I was afraid you'd see me looking, and I wasn't ready to say what you wanted to hear."

His hand fell away from her neck. "I don't want you to say only what I want to hear."

"That came out wrong," she said quickly. She began to fiddle nervously with the button of his shirt. "What I meant was that I wasn't ready to say what I felt, even though I knew it was what you wanted to hear."

"Why not?"

"I think," she said, "because things have happened so fast, and because what we have seems so...perfect...that I assumed there had to be a hitch."

"I thought you were an optimist."

"So did I. I guess I was nervous because nothing has ever meant so much to me before."

"Nothing?"

She shook her head. "Our relationship was like a dream. There were times when I knew that I wanted it to be forever, but I was afraid to think that way for fear of jinxing it."

"Superstitious, to boot?" he teased.

"No. Just dumb."

"What wised you up?"

"Missing you." She twisted the button back and forth. "And thinking about the struggles other couples go through." The backs of her fingers grazed his shirt, absorbing the warmth and strength of his body. "And realizing that I couldn't conceive of being with any other man but you."

"Caroline?" he asked in his softest voice.

"Mmm?"

"Why won't you look at me?"

She flattened her fingers over the button she'd been worrying. "I'm embarrassed."

"Because you've been crying?"

"No, because I've been a ninny. I'm supposed to know what I'm doing in situations like these. But I blew it."

"*Nearly* blew it," he corrected. The beginnings of a smile were in his voice and on his lips. "You've come to your senses in time."

Her head came up a little way, just enough so that she could focus on the pulse at his neck. "Then you forgive me for being dense?"

"On one condition."

Her eyes reached his mouth. "What's that?"

"That you stop taking the full responsibility for things that go wrong. You weren't the only one at fault here. We didn't talk. Neither of us. If I'd been open earlier about what I'd been thinking and feeling, I wouldn't have reached the point of frustration that I did."

"You're right," she said as her eyes touched his.

"I was a bastard to give you an ultimatum like that."

She considered that, then nodded. "You're right."

"Forgive me?"

"On one condition."

"Hmm?"

"The ultimatum sticks," she said with determination and promise. "It's either all or nothing. I've decided I want all. Can you give it?"

"Can I give it? Can I *give* it?" His eyes took on a breathtaking glow. "Oh-ho, baby, can I ever."

THAT NIGHT, Brendan wasn't wondering how much he could give but how much he could take. It was dark out. He stood before his window, staring across the courtyard into Caroline's loft. She was looking her seductive best, and it was driving him wild.

They had a date. They'd decided to dress up and go out for an elegant dinner to formally celebrate their love, but at the rate they were going, they'd never make it. Brendan was newly shaved and showered and had drawn on his dark suit pants, but those pants weren't feeling terribly comfortable at the moment. Fresh from her own shower, Caroline was leaning against the window jamb wearing nothing but a silk teddy. One of her arms was bent and braced against the wood by her head; the other rested loosely in the half lap she'd made by propping one knee on the window seat.

*Well?* he asked with a grin.

She returned the grin. *Well, what?*

*Are we going out?*

*Sure.*

His eyes made a sweep of her body, lingering at the swell of her breasts and the spot where her nipples pushed at the teddy. *You're not dressed.*

Her own appreciative eye wandered over his chest, leisurely following the tapering trail of hair to the spot where his pants waited to be fastened. *Neither are you.*

*I can't get dressed when you stand around that way. It distracts me.*

*You don't look distracted. You look attentive. And warm.*

*So do you,* he thought as she slowly brought her hand from her lap and curved it around her neck.

*Brendan?*

*Hmm?*

*When we buy our house, can we get one with air conditioning?*

*You bet.*

*I want four kids. Is that okay?*

*Of course it's okay. Caroline, please get dressed.*

*Do you play baseball?*

*Baseball? What does baseball have to do with anything?*

*I have this image of you coaching a Little League team.*

*Sweetheart, I will do anything, anything you want, if only you'll put something on. This is torture.*

Drawing her hand down her neck, she dipped two fingers into the hollow between her breasts. *I love you, brendan.*

*I love you, too, but if you don't get dressed soon, I won't be held responsible for my actions.*

*Do you really want to go out to dinner?*

*Caroline . . .*

She took a long, slow breath that expanded her rib cage and lifted her breasts. *We could call and put the reservations back an hour. . . .*

He blotted beads of sweat from his forehead with his arm.

She smiled. *I could fix you something to tide you over.*

*Tide me over? Ah, hell.* Backing away from the window, he thrust his feet into his loafers, grabbed his shirt and made for the door.

Across the courtyard, Caroline, too, backed away from the window. With a smug smile, she turned and started slowly across the room. Before she reached the door, she'd turned off every light in the loft except the small one by her bed. Then she opened the door and waited for Brendan.

# COMING NEXT MONTH

### #177 TEST OF TIME Jayne Ann Krentz

New bride Katy was thrilled by her husband's ardor and by the prospect of sharing a lifetime with him. Too soon she discovered the real reason Garrett had married her....

### #178 WIT AND WISDOM Shirley Larson

For a man whose lovemaking was more than eloquent, Joel was tongue-tied when it came to those three little words Alison longed to hear. It was high time to persuade him that words could speak as loudly as actions....

### #179 ONE OF THE FAMILY Kristine Rolofson

Allie had just popped into the post office to pick up a few letters—and ended up with one angry male! But even though her rambunctious kids had accidentally destroyed his bicycle, Michael quickly saw the advantages to being stranded....

### #180 BEFORE AND AFTER Mary Jo Territo

Verna Myers found the willpower to shed some pounds, and chose a spa to do the job. Then robust fellow guest Mel Hopkins made an unintentionally grand entrance into her life. And Verna suspected food would not be her only temptation....

# Sarah

## MAURA SEGER

Sarah wanted desperately to escape the clutches of her cruel father.
Philip needed a mother for his son, a mistress for his plantation.
It was a marriage of convenience.
Then it happened. The love they had tried to deny suddenly became a
blissful reality... only to be challenged by life's hardships and brutal
misfortunes.

---

**An intriguing story
of a love that defies the boundaries of time.**

*BEVERLY SOMMERS*

*Time and Again*

Knocked unconscious by a violent earthquake, Lauren,
a computer operator, wakes up to find that she is no
longer in her familiar world of the 1980s, but back in
1906. She not only falls into another era but also into
love, a love she had only known in her dreams.
Funny...heartbreaking...always entertaining.

# ATTRACTIVE, SPACE SAVING BOOK RACK

Display your most prized novels on this handsome and sturdy book rack. The hand-rubbed walnut finish will blend into your library decor with quiet elegance, providing a practical organizer for your favorite hard-or soft-covered books.

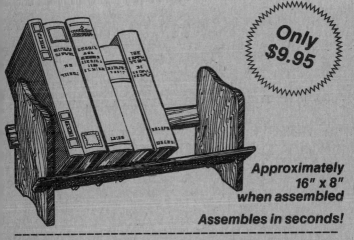

*Only $9.95*

***Approximately 16" x 8" when assembled***

***Assembles in seconds!***

---

To order, rush your name, address and zip code, along with a check or money order for $10.70* ($9.95 plus 75¢ postage and handling) payable to *Harlequin Reader Service*:

Harlequin Reader Service
Book Rack Offer
901 Fuhrmann Blvd.
P.O. Box 1396
Buffalo, NY 14269-1396

*Offer not available in Canada.*

BKR-1A

*New York and Iowa residents add appropriate sales tax.